GRACEFUL
Watercolors

Copyright ©2024 Heart-2-Heart Publishing LLC

Written by Suzette Riddick

All rights reserved. No part of this book may be reproduced or transmitted in any forms or means, electronic or mechanical, including photocopying, recording, or by any information storage and retrieval systems, without written permission from the publisher and author.

ISBN-13: 978-0982587157

This book is a work of fiction. Any reference to historical events, real people or real events is used fictitiously. Other names, characters, places, and events are products of the author's imagination and are not to be construed as real. Any resemblance to places, events, or real persons, living or dead, is purely coincidental.

Made in the United States of America

Cover Design: Jan Espanola, Ennel John Online Design

Project Editor: Nicole Falls, Trim & Polish Editing Services

Published by:

Heart-2-Heart Publishing LLC

P.O. Box 48186

Philadelphia, PA 19144

www.suzetteriddick.com

Also by Suzette Riddick

Generations Series
Wandering Beauty

Lawrence Family Series
Forever Yours
Fixer Upper Love
Finally Yours

Night Series
Caliente Nights
Sultry Nights
Seductive Nights

Two Hearts as One Series
Baby Love
Trembling Hearts
Mended Hearts

Love at Last Series
It's My Turn
Baby, I'm For Real

Love Conquers All Series
A Special Summer
When Love Comes Around
Key To My Heart
Second Chance At Love
The Sweetest Love

Anthologies

Losing The Bid

Chasing After Love

Dedication

I dedicate this book to my great-niece, Autumn Dorsey. I'm so proud of you and all you're accomplishing as a photographer for a professional NBA team. Love you, bunches!

GRACEFUL
Watercolors

SUZETTE RIDDICK

One

I'm tired of running. Emotionally, mentally, and physically, I am exhausted. It's time for me to go home. Permanently. Those were my thoughts as I watched my baby boy, Emanuel, sleeping. The stuffed dinosaur that was once snuggled against his chest while he slept precariously dangled off the edge of the bed. I supposed he continued to sleep with Charlie—that was the dinosaur's name—out of habit. Just as it was my habit to not deal with my problems head on.

Now my son favored toy trucks and building Lego dragons he played with for hours, entertaining himself. Manny, a nickname my grandfather gave him as an infant, claimed he was a big boy and ready to do away with his stuffed animals. But for some reason, Manny hung onto Charlie. This gave me hope because possibly my baby wasn't quite ready to relinquish being dependent on me. Because everything in me wished he would stay trapped in time so I could keep him sheltered from the harsh realities of our world. A world that one day *would* become his reality. Because of this inevitable certainty, it was time for me to stop running. And prepare myself, for once, to deal with the inescapable. Lately, there had been some invisible, indefinable thing I couldn't name that haunted me and I was scared. I supposed that was why I needed the sanctuary of where I came from.

Besides, it wasn't fair to Manny that I constantly uprooted him, traveling from place to place to escape my demons. My son was only seven years old and had traveled to most of the states and three continents. I owed it to him to settle down in one place where he would have a normal life, make friends his age, and hopefully build long lasting friendships like I had done with Jillian Hart and Kristen King.

As young children and teens the three of us dreamed big. Kristen and I would count down the months until Jillian returned to Colemanville for her summer vacation. Hours were spent at Copper Lake with the sun shining above us as we laid on a blanket gazing at the clear blue sky and fluffy clouds planning out our futures. We were going to grow up and do big things after college. Becoming independent women who would pave our own paths and live life on our terms. We were supposed to travel to places we learned about in school and read about in books and magazines. But things didn't happen that way. In college, I stuck to the script. I had a blast partying and exploring my sexuality with my boyfriend while I earned my degree in photography. Falling in love and having a baby hanging off my breast wasn't on my radar. Jillian and Kristen were the polar opposite. They found their happily-ever-after fairy tales. Adoring husbands and their bellies filled with babies was exchanged for our post-college graduation trip to Europe.

Not me though. In my eyes my best friends had settled for mundane lives while I'd chosen to go on about my life exploring all the things and traveling to places I'd fantasized about as a kid. In my idealism I'd believed the circle of people I'd surrounded myself with had my back and cared about me.

I loved Jillian and Kristen as if they were my flesh and blood, my sisters. As we grew apart, so did the bond that we once shared. As I jet-setted around the country and parts of the world, our friendship was tucked far away in a dark corner in the back of my mind. Years would go by before we made contact. Each time hollow promises were made to keep in touch.

When life did me dirty, I longed for Jillian and Kristen. Their shoulders to cry on. Their reassuring words to soothe my wounded soul. But I was too humiliated to let them know I was hurting. Instead, I put on a mask and pretended I had it all together, when really, I was drowning. And the only thing that kept me from being yanked beneath a sea of nothingness was the seed growing in my womb.

Shame nearly suffocated me when I thought about how I had lied to my best friends to conceal my secret. A secret that kept me dragging my sweet innocent baby from state to state, continent to continent, so I wouldn't have to confront my guilt. Or take accountability for my overzealousness to advance my career to be the next up and coming Black artist. And look where it had gotten me. A thousand times I scolded myself for walking away from my career as a photographer for the NBA. I had wanted to do more. To *be* more. I yearned to have my paintings and photographs hung on gallery walls. Sought out by wealthy art collectors. That was my driving force and it cost me way more than I had bargained to pay. The only thing that got me through was my mantra "give yourself grace" and putting one foot in front of the other to walk the path God had intended for me to walk. But had He intended for my path to be littered with stumbles, bumps, and bruises?

Manny stirring in his sleep pulled me out of my reverie. I studied his features that were so much like his father's. Everything from his light brown skin tone to his widow's peak and lanky limbs was Preston Jennings' genetic makeup. Every beat of my heart was for my son. My decision to keep him was never a second thought. The one thing I would change, if I could, would be who Manny's father was.

I ran my fingers through the soft loose curls on Manny's head before kissing his forehead. Preston was a mistake I wished I could go back and get a do over on. I would've walked the other way when he sauntered over to me at an art gallery that Sunday afternoon in Atlanta. I was too mesmerized by the renowned artist, who was put on the map after painting portraits of the Obama family and Maya Angelou before her passing, to see past his flattery. Overtaken by his satiny words that were as hollow as the chocolate Easter bunny I ate as a kid, I let my guard down.

Gently picking up Charlie, I placed him on the pillow next to Manny. Quietly, I left the room to go into the kitchen to pour myself a glass of wine before heading to my bedroom. Grabbing my phone off the nightstand, I called my sister Chantel. My temple throbbed as I waited for her to answer.

"Where are you off to now? And how long do I have to pack my bags?"

I laughed at Chantel's teasing. Four years younger than me, sometimes our roles were reversed and she was the big sister. If I hadn't had Chantel in my corner, I would've been somewhere wandering aimlessly. There was no way I would've been able to accept lucrative photography assignments that required me to jump on a plane at a moment's notice without my sister. Chantel's ability to work remotely as a graphic artist for a top-notch advertising firm allowed her to travel with me. Mind at ease, I was able to effectively do my job with her looking after my son.

"What makes you think I'm going somewhere?" I took a sip of my merlot, savoring its berry flavor.

"Oh...maybe because it's almost midnight and you're

usually in bed by now. And every time you call me to tell me you're off to some other place...you call late at night."

I rolled my eyes. Chantel was on point as usual. In my defense, Manny and I had been living in Nashville for almost two years where I taught photography at Nashville State Community College. It felt good having a routine for Manny. But I wanted more than a routine for my child. I wanted him to be immersed in community and family. As a kid I hadn't appreciated elderly neighbors telling me their childhood stories passed down to them about Cain Robertson, one of the founders of Colemanville of whom I was a direct descendent. Or being reminded that Chantel and I inherited our love for art and photography from our great-grandmother Ilona Robertson-Thurman, our maternal grandfather's mother. I certainly hadn't cherished my friendship with Kristen and Jillian.

"I'm going back home, Chantel."

Silence hung in the air. I knew what Chantel was thinking. Once I went away to college, I swore I would never go back to Colemanville to live. Once, twice a year to visit my parents and grandparents was all Colemanville, North Carolina would see of me.

"You're done with traveling? I thought you were going to Chicago next."

"I'm tired of moving, Chantel. I want stability for Manny."

"Then Colemanville is where you should be."

Two

It was bittersweet leaving my job as a photography instructor. I was going to miss teaching, especially the students who had a zeal for photography and viewed it as a serious artform. By the end of the semester, the serious students usually expressed a desire to further their education in the art. Careful not to give out my personal information, I set up a photography Facebook group where I could keep in touch with former students to continue mentoring them.

I had been back in Colemanville for three weeks. To my surprise, Manny hadn't adapted as well as I thought he would. The first week he cried and was withdrawn, downright miserable. No amount of consoling seemed to help ease his sadness.

"Mommy, why we had to leave home? I want to go back so I can play with my friends."

Manny referring to Nashville as home had me wondering if I made the right decision moving back to Colemanville. Especially since I had pulled him out of school in the middle of the school year to attend Profit Coleman Elementary School. Maybe I should've waited until the end of the school year like Chantel had suggested. In my eagerness, I wanted to get to Colemanville as fast as the next flight would get me there. My mother having a property available for rent was a factor that propelled my decision to move quickly.

"Manny, Mommy promise, this is the last time we're going to move."

The doubtful look in his dark brown eyes broke my heart. I didn't blame my baby boy for being skeptical. All I could do was show him we were here to stay. No more hastily packing some things and leaving others behind to move on to the next location.

Thankfully, as the days passed, so did his sullen mood. I had my neighbor Jenny who lived three doors down to thank. Her little Noah was the same age as Manny. The boys became fast friends. Manny was back to his playful self, blessed with the energy of three boys his age, wearing me out.

"What are you going to do about a job?"

The prying inquiry drew me out of my musing. I glanced up from the bowl of clam chowder I was savoring to look at my mom, Rosaline Caswell. My brows furrowed at her question. I couldn't tell if she was being condescending or not. Although I was a successful freelance photographer, my mother made it no secret that she still held resentment over the fact that I hadn't gone into the real estate business with her. As her eldest child it was my duty to work side by side with her. Chantel was never held to the same standard as me when it came to the expectations of how I lived my life. My mother saw it solely as my responsibility to grab the baton to keep her real estate business going forward into the next generation. I loved my mother, but she could be a bully. And I wasn't having it. This talk about a job was going to weave its way into working for her. *Never.*

Throughout the years, I'd done well with saving and investing money. A few of my paintings and photographs had sold for a decent amount. In addition to my last position as a photography instructor, I rented out studio space and did photoshoots as a side hustle. Mostly maternity, newborn, and wedding photos, which paid extremely well. Word of mouth was a powerful tool. People traveled across state lines to book a session with me. The first week I arrived back to Colemanville, I updated my website and social media pages. Unfortunately, without a space to work, I couldn't take on a full booking of clients. Hence inviting my mom out to lunch.

"That's why I asked you out to lunch," I began slowly, looking my mother in the eyes.

Mom perked up, setting her salad fork down beside her plate. "You're finally ready to help me run the business?"

For a second, I wanted to challenge my mom as to why she never looked to Chantel to step up to work for the business. It was wasted energy. I kept my irritation to myself because I needed something from her. Mom was a bully, not spiteful. But that didn't mean I wanted to sit here and listen to her go on and on about her legacy dying with her. Oh yes, she played the guilt card too.

As soon as I said, "No, Mom," her shoulders sagged. "Dad told me some time ago you purchased the old catering hall. I was wondering if I could rent it. I'd like to turn the downstairs into a studio and art gallery. And use the upstairs for me and Manny's living quarters."

"Your father talks too much."

I couldn't help laughing at my mom's grumbling. My parents divorced when I was fourteen. I never fully understood the reasoning. It wasn't as if they were always at each other's throat. An occasional argument here or there was witnessed between them. Certainly nothing that had prepared me and my sister for them sitting us down to tell us they were dissolving their marriage after fifteen years. All either of them would divulge was that they were no longer compatible. Whatever that meant. Throughout the years they both dated, but neither remarried, which Chantel and I found interesting.

"Do you have any plans for the building?" I tried to keep my tone even and not reveal my desperation.

Picking her fork back up, Mom speared a cherry tomato. "No, I don't have plans for it. I suppose I can rent it to you..." She gave me a crooked grin. "Since it'll be home to my grandson, I'll give you a decent discount on the rent."

Scooting my chair back, I didn't care about the other patrons gawking our way as I went to my mother. I gave her a tight hug. "Thanks, Mom. I appreciate you."

Mom's hug was just as tight. I was sure she was taken aback by me being affectionate. Sadly, we never had that kind of relationship.

"You're welcome, baby. Come by the office tomorrow so I can give you the keys. It's pretty messy in there. You'll have to hire a trash removal company to clean the place out. I have the perfect company that's not too expensive. Do you have enough money? Or will you have to take out a loan?"

"One of my paintings sold for a decent amount a few months ago. I have enough savings that should get me through the next six months."

"Six months, Ella?"

Mom choked on the sweet tea she was drinking. Clearing her throat, she wiped at the corners of her mouth with the white cloth napkin on her lap. "What happens after the six months are up?"

Mentally I counted down from ten. Since I'd been on my own, I'd never once called home for money or missed paying rent. Were there times when things were lean and instead of taking Manny out to the movies I rented a DVD from a local Redbox and served him microwave popcorn? Absolutely. But neither me nor my child had ever gone hungry, been without a roof over our heads, or without utilities.

"Mom, I'm going to be fine. I've had to turn business away and I'm already booked for five weddings so far this spring and summer. Tomorrow I was planning on putting up flyers at the library on the bulletin board advertising maternity and newborn photoshoots."

Satisfied with my answer, Mom laid her napkin back on her lap. "If you say so." She gave me a skeptical look. "How much do people pay for those maternity photoshoots? They're in all the magazines and online. That wasn't a thing when I was pregnant with you and Chantel."

I covered my mouth as I chewed my sandwich I'd just bitten into. "Anywhere from five hundred to twelve hundred. Depending on what the client wants. And how long the photoshoot is."

"Is that sustainable income?"

Why was she acting like I'm new at this?

"Don't worry, Mom. I'm good enough at what I do to make a living to take care of me and my son."

I stopped eating to hold my breath. Her gaze studied me as if I was a rare piece of art.

"You're my child, Ella Marie Caswell. No matter how old you get, I'm always going to worry about you."

Mom's prickly attitude had never stood in the way of loving me although we seemed to be at odds on most things. I never understood, until I became a mother, the depth of what it was to worry about another human being.

"I know, Mom. Believe me, I know."

Three

My maternal grandparents, Xavier and Rose Thurman, lived on a beautiful, tree-lined street four blocks from where Manny and I were currently living. It didn't take much convincing for Manny to abandon his Lego set to take a walk to visit our grandparents. Their only great-grandchild, Xavier and Rose adored the ground Manny walked on. Manny adored them too. Mostly because there was always a sweet treat waiting for him. On any given day it could be homemade ice cream, sticky buns, cupcakes, or cookies. We never left without Grandma Rose packing up a shopping bag loaded with goodies before we headed home.

Hand in hand, we strolled down the street taking in the sights. A lazy cat sunbathing on a porch. Bushy-tailed squirrels scurrying up and down trees. Bumblebees did their pollinating thing as they buzzed from flower to flower. I slowed down, wishing I had my Nikon Z8 to snap a few pictures. After Manny was fast asleep, I could've unwound by breaking out my watercolor paper pad to create a replica of nature. I had just gotten around to reading Preston's email from several days ago via my website because I didn't want to be bothered. His demanding my whereabouts had left my nerves on edge. Every other year he took a hiatus from his jet-setting life as an artist to "check in on" his son. Out of the seven years Manny has been alive, Preston had seen him four times. Chantel swore Preston popping in and out of our lives was to control me. If she only knew.

I pushed thoughts of Preston out of my brain to languish in my surroundings. It seemed everyone had a thing for rose or honeysuckle bushes. One of the things I loved about Colemanville was the clean, fragrant air from the flowering bushes. I inhaled deeply to drag the scent into my lungs, cleansing my insides.

"How was school today, Manny?"

Lifting his head to gaze at me, Manny squinted against the late afternoon sun. "I guess okay." He hunched his shoulders, looking away from me.

"Why just okay?"

"Stupid Amanda was taking too long to show her stupid doll at show and tell. And there wasn't enough time for me to show my picture of us on the camel."

The picture he was referring to was from when I was hired to do a seven-day photoshoot in Giza, Egypt. Before leaving for the freelance job, Chantel and I planned to stay a few extra days after I was done working to explore. Manny inherited my adventurous spirit. The folks in our tour group were astounded that at five he wasn't afraid of the camels. Probably because my baby kept calling the camels "big ponies." The previous summer, Granddad X had taken him over to Sims Stables to ride the ponies. Meeting Noah, and a promise to take them to the stables once school was out for summer break, seemed to be the turning point for Manny accepting our new home.

I turned my head so I could silently laugh before I

addressed my child calling his classmate stupid. I imagined him scrunching up his forehead in aggravation with little Amanda at school today. Doing my best to put on a stern face, I tugged Manny's hand so he would look back up at me. "Manny, you know it's not nice to call people names...right?"

He dropped his head. "Yes, Mommy."

"Will there be a show and tell next Friday at school?"

Manny nodded, swinging his free arm. "Yes. My teacher said I can go first."

When I ruffled his curls with my fingers, he smiled at me. "See, problem solved, Mr. Manny."

My baby's cherub grin was precious. "Yep."

As we came to a stop at the corner, a shiny, red classic convertible Mustang pulled up to the red light. Whoever the owner was, I could tell they took pride in the vehicle by the way it was highly polished from the car's frame to the jet-black tires. The classic car reminded me of Mr. Harvey's 1967 Mustang. One summer during our crazy teen years, me, Jillian, and Kristen "borrowed" Mr. Harvey's Mustang to go joyriding while he and his wife were away on a cruise to the Caribbean. Kristen worked that summer at Mr. Harvey's auto shop as a receptionist. She had access to the building and knew where he kept an extra set of keys to the vehicle.

We would not have gotten caught if Jillian hadn't decided to blast Will Smith rapping about Summertime as we cruised down Fig Avenue thinking we were cute. No amount of crying and pleading dissuaded the sheriff from piling us up in the backseat of his cruiser and hauling us off to the jailhouse. It was Nana Flo, Jillian's grandmother, who told our parents to leave us in jail overnight. We were better off staying in jail. Nana Flo showed up the next morning with a belt and tore our behinds up.

"Mommy! Look at that car!"

Manny's new fascination I discovered last week in Target

while we were in the toy aisle were Matchbox cars. He seemed to have an affinity for the classic style cars. Whenever Manny expressed an interest in something, I would go down a rabbit hole in search of his latest obsession. Mostly because it gave me ideas for stocking stuffers for Christmas and birthday gifts. I was still trying to decide if that was a good or bad thing. Sometimes I struggled with not giving him whatever he expressed interest in.

Before I could stop him, Manny broke away from me and ran up to the driver's side. "Hi, mister. I like your car."

Oh no. Manny's hands were plastered on the door. I was sure his fingerprints were going to be visible once he removed his grimy little hands.

"Manny, please get over here."

The driver, a handsome man with dark, shoulder length locs, lifted his shades to gaze at Manny and it took my breath away. Other than my father and grandfather, I had never witnessed another man look at my son that way. The stranger's dark eyes held tenderness that Preston had never displayed when looking at my son. God help me. He turned those eyes on me and our gazes connected. A path of warmth flowed from the roots of my curly afro to the tips of my toenails. The upturned grin at the corners of his mouth was giving me palpitations.

Obediently, Manny eased away from the classic vehicle to stand at my side. Sure enough, ten tiny fingerprints were left behind. Not knowing what to do, I grabbed Manny's hand to ground me.

"No harm done, Miss." He turned his gaze back to Manny. It should've made me glad that his attention was taken off me, but it left me *wanting* his attention. Attention, until now, I had avoided at all cost.

"Thank you, Manny. Do you know what kind of car this is?"

It didn't slide past me that he called my son by his name.

Manny dug his hand into the khaki cargo pants he was wearing, producing a toy car.

"Is it this one?"

I wanted to tell the man behind the wheel that the light had changed and he should be moving along. But I couldn't. Not when Manny was so excited.

"Let me see that."

Manny released my hand to drop the toy in the center of the man's palm. Lips pursed, he rotated the blue car in his hand. "Naw, this is a Porsche. What I'm driving is a 1967 convertible Mustang."

Mr. Harvey's car was a 1967 Mustang of the same color. What were the chances?

A car pulled up behind the Mustang and honked its horn. Stepping forward, I pulled Manny back. "We don't want to hold you."

Putting the sunglasses back on, he grinned at Manny. "See you around, Manny. Hope to see you later, pretty lady."

"Bye, mister!" If Manny didn't stop waving his hand so hard, it was possible it might snap in two.

Tongue tied, my wave wasn't anywhere as enthusiastic as Manny's.

He honked the horn before taking off, headed to wherever he was going. Manny and I stood rooted in place until the shiny, red car was no longer visible.

Four

Manny ran up the five wooden stairs leading onto the front porch of my grandparents' home. The deliciously sweet aroma of something tasty baking wafted through the screen door, tickling my nostrils. Honest to goodness, my grandmother was the best baker in all of Colemanville. At every church event where food was going to be served someone always requested her famous peach cobbler and pecan pie.

"Grandma Rose! Granddad X! I'm here!"

There was no use in me telling Manny to slow down as he announced himself and took off charging in the direction of the kitchen.

Like a magnet I was drawn to the mantel above the fireplace lined with photos of Granddad X's parents, Ilona and Gabe, along with photos of my grandparents in their younger years. Reverently, I picked up the ornate brass picture frame with Ilona and Gabe sitting on a park bench with the Eiffel Tower in the distance. Whoever took the photo was one heck of a skilled photographer. Their ability to capture the essence of my great-grandparents' affection for one another was mesmerizing. The longing in their eyes was undeniable. As a young teen I would gaze at the photo and fantasize about one day finding my Prince Charming like Ilona had done with Gabe.

I knew it was silly, but when I went to Paris I searched for that park bench until I thought I had found it. Camera on a strap around my neck, some tourists thought I was a weirdo, while others indulged me when I approached them to ask if I could take a photo of them. Those who were kind enough to humor me, allowed me to position them on the park bench sitting close facing each other with the man's arm draped over the woman's shoulder and the woman's hand resting on her guy's thigh. I would instruct them to gaze lovingly into each other's eyes. Some I was able to capture a spark of love, others not so much. No matter my efforts, I could never recreate that magic between Ilona and Gabe in the photo.

"I should just go on and give you that picture."

A smile tugged at the corners of my mouth. Reverently, I returned the photo back to its resting place amongst the others.

"You should. It would be the kind thing to do."

Granddad X embraced me tightly when I turned to hug him. "You know I love that picture."

Releasing me, my grandfather held his arm out in the true fashion of a southern gentleman. I looped my arm through his. He slowly led me to the kitchen.

"Why don't you paint a portrait of it? That way you'll always have it."

It wasn't unusual of Granddad X to issue such a challenge. My gaze landed on the oil portrait above the sofa. It was a recreation of my grandparents' wedding photo I had painted as a gift for their fiftieth wedding anniversary celebration. Everyone marveled at how it was nearly a perfect replica of the original photograph.

I'd thought about painting that photo of my great-grandparents at least a hundred times. But never followed through out of fear I wouldn't do it justice. My great-grandmother Ilona was an amazing artist who defied her first husband and parents to pursue her art. Years after I had painted the anniversary gift, Chantel and I came across one of Ilona's paintings in an art museum in Nice, France. I stood staring at that painting so long that Chantel left me to explore the other paintings and photographs in the museum. The painting was of a small male child running in an open pasture. Mesmerized by the vibrant brush strokes of blues, yellows, and greens, I had felt somehow connected to the painting. I could remember wondering what was happening during Ilona's life at the time she had created that piece. From the movement of the painting and the bold hues, I had guessed she was content.

"Or you could just give me the photo." I tilted my head to gaze up at my granddad adoringly like I did as a child.

Granddad X reminded me I was no longer an adorable, pigtail-wearing kid. "No way, Missy. It's my favorite picture of Mama and Daddy. If you want it, you paint it. Besides, your sister loves that picture too. Wouldn't be fair to give it to you."

I didn't want to sass my granddad by telling him nowadays you could make duplicates of photos. Duplicates weren't the same as the originals though, in my opinion. Chantel and I rarely dabbled in sibling rivalry. However, we would when it came to that photo. There was no way as the oldest, I would settle for a duplicate. That photo was my birthright.

Grandma Rose was placing a glass of milk beside a plate containing two large sugar cookies in front of Manny when we entered the kitchen.

"Thank you, Grandma Rose."

"You're welcome, sweet baby."

My grandmother kissed Manny's forehead and it melted my heart, chasing away my doubts. Miles away, Manny and I wouldn't be able to decide on a whim to put on our tennis shoes and walk a few blocks over to see my parents or grandparents.

"What were you two in there yapping about?"

Granddad X and I peeped at each other before we started laughing.

Tickled, I asked, "How do you know we were yapping?"

Grandma Rose clucked her tongue. "Because y'all were taking too long to get in here." She tapped her ears. "Got my hearing aids in."

Growing up, I was reserved with most people until I knew them well. Grandma Rose swore it was because my grandfather was my first buddy. Apparently, I preferred my grandfather's company and would follow him out back to the shed where he did carpentry work. Deemed an unsafe place for a two-year-old, Mom would run behind me and attempt to take me back inside. Grandma Rose said I would kick and scream something terrible. "Had the neighbors thinking we were over here whipping you. Xavier had to keep the shed doors wide open."

My great-grandparents Ilona and Gabe were living with my grandparents by that time. I was told Ilona and Gabe would sit at a distance from the shed, each alternating between holding me on their laps while I watched Granddad X work.

I wished I could remember such precious memories. All that was left were photos of me and Chantel with our great-grandparents. Sadly, Gabe died in his sleep at the age of ninety-seven when I was eight years old. Ilona joined her beloved the following spring. Even as a child I comprehended my grandfather's grief of losing both of his parents within such a close time span. It drew me closer to him. I do remember being snuggled against him for hours watching old Western movies. Grandma Rose had praised me for comforting my grandfather through his grief.

"Rose, this here thorn in my side was pestering me for Mama and Daddy's picture...again."

"Ha! Thorn in your side, my foot. The two of you are two peas in a pod."

Playfully, I rolled my eyes. I was anything but a thorn. More like the twinkle in his eyes. Ignoring my grandfather's jab, I went over to my grandmother to love on her.

Grandma Rose was a tiny, little thing. At my height of five-six, her head rested below my chin when I hugged her petite frame.

"Hey, Grandma Rose. How's it going?"

"Pretty good, nothing extra. You doing okay?"

Her question made me feel uneasy. Especially with her gazing at me as if trying to decipher if I was going to tell her the truth or not.

"I'm good. Just wanted to get Manny out of the house for a walk. Get some exercise and fresh air."

Granddad X shuffled past Manny, ruffling his full head of sandy brown curls as he made his way to the refrigerator. Manny tilted his head back, mouth full of cookies to grin at his great-grandfather. "Hi, Granddad X."

My son quickly covered his mouth when I raised a brow at him. Nothing got on my nerves like someone talking with a mouth full of food.

"Manny, got any exciting news for me?" Granddad X inquired while rooting through the refrigerator.

Digging in his pocket, Manny pulled out the matchbox car. "Me and Mommy saw a car that looked like this." Manny frowned. "Except the man said it wasn't the same kind of car."

My mouth started watering at the sight of the platter of fried fish covered in clear saran wrap, even though Manny and I ate before leaving home.

Granddad X set the platter on the table and picked up the toy car, inspecting it. "Is that so?"

Nodding his head toward the countertop, he said, "I'mma heat us up some of this here fish in that there contraption."

That there contraption was an air fryer.

"Mommy, what kind of car did the man say it was?"

Before I could answer, Grandma Rose butted in. She gave me a sly smile as if anticipating a juicy secret. "What man?"

Grandma Rose was one of those old school women who believed a good man made everything alright. I supposed in her case it did. Grandma Rose was orphaned at twelve and shipped down south to live with a relative in Colemanville. She and my great auntie Jessica were classmates and became best friends. One day Grandma Rose showed up to school with a black eye and busted lip. The relative's husband demanded payment for eating his food and sleeping under his roof. When Grandma Rose refused to do things no twelve-year-old should be expected to do with a grown man, he roughed her up pretty badly.

Ilona took one look at Grandma Rose and told Gabe she wouldn't let her go back to that den of demons. It didn't matter that they had four children of their own to care for and would be taking on another mouth to feed. Story went, as Grandma Rose had begun to blossom, Granddad X became smitten with her. No longer viewing his younger sister's friend as a kid. One lingering glance turned to two. Before long, my grandparents were teenaged bride and groom. Seven months later, my mother, Rosaline, was born.

I supposed that was why my grandparents hadn't judged me when I got pregnant with Manny. The only complaint they had was that Preston hadn't done the honorable thing in their eyes by marrying me.

"Just some man in a red sports car." Casually, I headed over to the counter to see what Granddad X was over there doing with the air fryer. He had the setting up way too high. I turned it down to prevent the fish from burning to a crisp.

Not letting up, Grandma Rose shuffled over to the fridge and grabbed a Tupperware container I was hoping contained her potato salad.

"Was he good looking? You know my Xavier was the best-looking fella in Colemanville."

Even Manny tittered when Granddad X grumbled, "Woman, what you talkin' 'bout was? I'm still the best-looking fella in Colemanville."

"He was okay looking."

Now that was a big, fat lie. The man was handsome and captivating with a smile that could chase the storm clouds away.

I shooed my granddad away from the air fryer. "Sit down, good looking. I got this. You too, good looking lady."

Heading to the sink, I washed my hands and dried them as I went about gathering plates and silverware. While I worked at setting the table, I half-listened to my grandparents making plans to take Manny to Sims Stables in a few weeks when school let out. Somehow, Preston's email made its way to the forefront of my mind. I knew if I didn't respond to him soon, he'd be irritated enough to pick up the phone and call. I detested talking to him. It literally made my skin crawl. Afterwards, I would have to shower to feel clean.

My mind was not focused on what I was doing. Instead of grabbing an oven mitt to remove the rack the fish was on, I picked up a dish towel.

"Got dang it!" The thinner fabric was no match for the hot rack. I dropped the rack, sending fish flying over the countertop.

"You okay, Mommy?"

I gritted my teeth through the pain. "I'm okay, baby."

Grandma Rose made haste to stand beside me at the sink. She turned the cold water on and gently shoved my hand under the running stream.

"Xavier, bring some ice over here."

Granddad X was already at the ice dispenser on the refrigerator door. Manny came over to me, wrapping his skinny arms around my waist. He tilted his head back to gaze at me. I could see the anxiety in his dark eyes. I blinked several times to keep my tears at bay. Something in the tone of Preston's email didn't sit well with my spirit. Why wouldn't he leave us alone? No, not us. Me?

"Mommy, why you look sad?"

The dam broke, spilling bitter tears. "Because Mommy is sad."

Five

"I'm catching the next flight I can book."

In the dark, I sat Indian style on the floor with my back against the sofa. Granddad X and Grandma Rose tried their best to comfort me. To get me to open up about what I had kept bottled up for eight years. I couldn't bring myself to uncover my secret. It was one of those secrets that every now and again gave reprieve. Allowing me to catch my breath and breathe. Only for its hateful tentacles to slither around my soul, suffocating me. Would they think some way, somehow, I was to blame? I knew Granddad X and Grandma Rose loved me. Even at my big age they adored me. Part of me didn't take that affection for granted. In the back of my mind, I believed they would view me through a different lens. I didn't know if I would be able to live with them looking at me differently. So I kept my mouth shut and dried my tears.

After Manny was bathed and put to bed, I got my laptop and pulled up Preston's email again. Three times, I read it. Each time it came across more ominous than the last.

I came by your place to see my son. Your neighbor said you moved months ago. I'm sick of this little game you're determined to play. Ella you better remember... I always win.

A chill ran through me every time I read it. Scared, I called Chantel and read her the email. My fear deepened when she agreed Preston's tone was threatening.

"You don't have to do that, Chantel."

"I know I don't. But I can tell something else is bothering you, Ella. I can hear it all in your voice and I don't like it. I know one thing, Preston better think hard before he tries something."

Booking a flight at the last minute was going to be outrageously expensive. But she was right. I needed her because I felt in every fiber of my being that Preston was up to no good.

"Are you sure?" As much as I wanted my sister here with me, it did bother me that I was once again intruding into her life.

"Of course. I booked the flight as soon as I heard what that *thing* wrote to you. Besides, I haven't been home in ages. It would be good to see everyone." I could see her grinning when she reminded me, "You know I'm Grandma Rose's favorite."

"And I'm Granddad X's. So that makes us even."

Chantel's melodious laughter coming through the phone comforted me.

"What time is your flight landing? I can come get you."

Glancing at the time on my phone, it was a little after eleven. Chantel was flying out of New York and the closest airport was in Fayetteville, which was almost an hour from Colemanville. Chantel probably wouldn't be here until morning, depending on what time her flight departed.

The background noise was all too familiar to me. Chantel was moving about, throwing clothing and necessities in her favorite enormous vintage black leather Gucci duffle bag she picked up on our last shopping spree to What Goes Around Comes Around years ago when we were in Soho. I wanted to tell her to pack a large suitcase instead because I wanted her to stay with me indefinitely. Selfish of me, I knew.

"I can get an Uber or call Dad and ask him to pick me up. I don't want you dragging my nephew out of bed. You know how cranky he can get."

Unlike our mother, our father wouldn't pry with a million questions, insisting on knowing why Chantel had jumped on a plane in the middle of the night to come be with me.

Before I could suggest that she take an Uber, Chantel beat me to it. "Forget it. I'll get an Uber because if Mom finds out Dad picked me up she going to start in with her—"

"You've always liked your father better than me," we said at the same time while laughing.

It wasn't that we liked our father better. Our dad was laid back and didn't tend to be as controlling as our mom. With Dad, he gave us latitude to voice our opinions and even disagree with him when we believed his stance was too strict. With Mom, we had no choice but to be in compliance with what she decreed. "Young lady, it's my house, my rules. Do what you want when you're grown," was dished out to me and Chantel as we became teens.

"Ella, get some sleep. I'll be there soon."

The knock on the door jarred me from my restless sleep. Beautiful hues of pink, yellow, orange, and red peeked at me through the sheer curtains as I bolted up. Heart racing, I ran the short distance to the door. There she was. Duffle bag thrown over her shoulder. Cardboard coffee holder with two cups of coffee in one hand and a white bag in the other with some sort of pastry, I was sure.

I couldn't control the crack in my voice. "You're here."

"I'm here."

Chantel had to adjust how she was holding the coffee from the way I was clinging onto her. She had no idea how she was my lifeline right now. We stood that way for the longest until Chantel gently pulled away.

"Sis, believe it or not, this coffee is starting to feel like I'm holding a pile of bricks."

"Oh! I'm sorry. Give it to me."

Chantel dropped her duffle bag in front of the sofa before following me into the kitchen. Glancing around, she took in the three-bedroom bungalow style home.

"This place is cute. You sure you don't want to stay here instead of living over the studio?"

Careful not to spill the coffee, I removed the lids so I could heat our drinks up in the microwave. I spoke loud enough for her to hear me as she perused my space.

"Granddad X and Grandma Rose asked me the same thing. I'm thinking about reconsidering."

My grandparents had pointed out that although it would have been convenient to live above the studio, it probably wouldn't be a wise decision to do so. "Ella, it might not be safe for your clients to know where you live," Grandma Rose had pointed out.

"I think you should. You have this place decorated so homey. Be right back, gotta use the bathroom. Which way?"

"Upstairs, second door on the left."

By the time Chantel came back downstairs, I was on the sofa. Our drinks were on the coffee table and our pastries—an apple turnover for me and a cherry for Chantel—on saucers. My stomach was a jittery mess when she sat down beside me so close that we resembled conjoined twins. Now that Chantel was here, I didn't want to dredge up the past. Content to have her with me, her presence made me feel safe.

"Ella, as Grandma Rose would say, it's time for you to do some house cleaning."

I nodded and inhaled deeply. As I exhaled, my eight-year secret poured out like a spilled glass of water flowing freely.

Six

Photography paid the bills but it was painting that made my soul sing. If I had my way, I would've made an attempt at painting for a living. But when you had a mother like mine who made every attempt to strong-arm you into following in her footsteps to have what she called "a profitable career" anyone would've done what I did.

I grew to love photography because it was a hobby of my grandfather's that we bonded over. Although Granddad X knew my passion was painting and that I someday wanted to be known in the Black circle of artists as his mother, Ilona Robertson-Thurman, had been known, he encouraged a broader path. Even let me in on a little secret. My great-grandmother's first love was photography, but she was discouraged to follow her dream and instead became a painter.

It was Granddad X's gentle way of urging me to apply for a photo management internship with the NBA while I was in my junior year of college. That internship led to me being a team photographer with the New York Knicks the following year when I graduated. Although I enjoyed traveling from city to city, I counted down the days until the season was over.

Between seasons I'd lock myself in my studio apartment in North New Jersey and paint for hours. For my grandmother's birthday, I shipped her a painting of a little girl gazing in the window of a candy store. She encouraged me to submit the painting to the Nubian-Kush Collaborative, an organization that supported Black artists and offered fellowships to study art abroad and at home in the States. Although I didn't win the fellowship, I wasn't deterred from pursuing my dream.

Whenever I traveled with the Knicks, I sought out art museums that featured Black art and artists. After the team played the Hawks in Atlanta, I stayed behind to go to an exhibit at a museum featuring Preston Jennings' work. I had studied Jacob Lawrence's work in college and was excited to see Preston's work up close and personal. Many referred to him as the contemporary version of Jacob Lawrence. Preston also used blacks and browns juxtaposed with bold colors in his paintings. I was standing in front of a canvas of a gorgeous, deep brown skinned woman in a red dress with her hands held high releasing a white dove toward a beautiful blue sky. The expression on her face was pure bliss.

"Sometimes I wish I could fly away like that dove."

Enraptured by the painting, I was startled by the deep timbre of the male voice behind me. Naturally, I swung around to see who had scared the mess out of me. I found myself face to face with the artist. Nervous, my heart pounded heavily in my chest. His mixed heritage of Black and Portuguese made him an interestingly handsome specimen. The sandy brown, low-cut curls covering his head were a shade lighter than his eyes. In print his average sized frame appeared taller than his actual height of five-eleven.

He chuckled when I continued to stare at him dumbfounded which caused me to laugh too.

Finding my tongue, I somewhat agreed with him. "I think most of us feel that way sometimes."

The crooked grin he gave me made me woozy. "I think you're right."

I wish I had never taken his outstretched hand. "Preston Jennings."

Usually, I wasn't a flirt. That time I was as I coyly smiled at him. "I know who you are, Mr. Jennings. I'm Ella Caswell."

Preston held onto my hand longer than was necessary.

"You submitted a piece for the Nubian-Kush Collaborative a few years ago."

I tilted my head to stare at him. "How'd you know that?"

"I was on the board and privy to all the submissions. Thought you would've won since your great-grandmother Ilona Robertson-Thurman was an outstanding artist and served on the board before her passing."

I remembered being impressed he knew of my great-grandmother's legacy.

"Not necessarily. I was happy for the young lady who was awarded the fellowship. She earned it fair and square."

Others had gathered around Preston to speak to him, prompting me to move along to view other pieces in his collection. As I moved from painting to painting, I could feel his eyes on me. Before I left to go back to my hotel within walking distance from the museum, Preston caught up with me before I made it out the glass doors.

"You were going to leave without saying goodbye?"

"I was. I have a plane to catch in the morning."

"Where are you staying?"

"Not far," was all I said. But it didn't deter Preston. He left his exhibit to walk me to the lobby of the hotel where I was staying. Before parting ways, he asked for my number. I gave it to him, figuring he probably wouldn't call. But he did call.

We developed a friendship over calls, texts, and emails. He lived in Atlanta, making it easy for us to meet for lunch or dinner whenever I came to town with the team. On one of those occasions, we went back to his home studio. I couldn't resist when he offered to show me what he was working on. In a moment of optimism, I blurted, "Someday I'd like to exhibit my work." It wasn't to suggest a handout or anything. I was just caught up in the possibility of my dream of being a well-known artist becoming a reality.

Preston had moved up so close behind me as I was admiring his latest piece that I could feel the sexual energy radiating off of him. A shiver passed through me when he murmured in my ear, "I can help you...if you're serious."

When I turned to thank him, he kissed me and the room started spinning. Immediately, my mind raced, trying to figure out how I was going to get out of a situation that suddenly was going left. Extracting myself from his hold, I backed up. The stunned expression on my face must've given him pause. "I'm sorry, Ella. I shouldn't've done that."

He bought my excuse of having to get back to my hotel because I had a five a.m. flight to catch back to New York for work. It felt like I held my breath until I was back inside my hotel room. My admiration for Preston as an artist kept me from blurring the lines by becoming romantically involved with him. Yes, initially, I was attracted to him. But I didn't want that from him. A week or so passed by before he sent me a text asking if we could talk.

"Ella, I want to apologize again. I know I was out of line. I hope it doesn't stop you from allowing me to assist you with showcasing your work at a friend's gallery."

I was hesitant in my answer. "Preston, I don't know. I view you as a mentor, not someone I want to have a romantic relationship with."

His chuckle was lighthearted. "Ouch!"

I laughed too. "The truth is, Preston, I haven't been in a

relationship for a long time because it's not something I want at this time in my life. I'm interested in my art...that's it."

"Understood."

And I thought he had understood. Because like nothing had ever happened, Preston and I picked back up where we left off before the awkward kiss. He and Victoria Clare, his friend who owned an art gallery, flew to New York to see my work in person. I'd been working on a collection titled *Colemanville*. One summer I was in Granddad X's work shed and came across a box containing photographs Ilona had taken around town during the nineteen forties. Captivated, I pleaded with my grandfather to part with several of the photos. I had completed watercolor paintings of Copper Lake, Fig Avenue, and Grayson's Mercantile from my great-grandmother's photos.

"These are breathtaking," Victoria gushed, reaching out as if she was going to touch the painting of Copper Lake. "Makes you want to lie down on the lush green grass."

"I'm doing an exhibit to feature new artists in June. Do you think you can do two more paintings for a collection of five to put on exhibit?"

Excited, I grabbed Preston's hand. "Yes!" I hadn't cared that I would have to share the spotlight with others. Just as long as some of that light shone on me.

The exhibit was a success. My family showed up to support me. Preston charmed everyone, especially when he announced I was the great-granddaughter of Ilona Robertson-Thurman. I glanced over at my granddad and would never forget the emotional tears in his eyes from the applause at the mention of his mother's name. My relation to Ilona had sold two paintings. I had felt honored to stand in the shadow of my great-grandmother's legacy. By the end of the night, two paintings were left. Victoria requested that I leave one of them in the gallery for her to sell. "I want to show you off as a new and upcoming artist."

After the showing my family and I, along with Preston and Victoria, went out to dinner to celebrate my success. Preston inserted himself to sit beside me. Giddy, I didn't pay attention to his arm casually draped over the back of my chair, making it appear as though we were more than friends. I had relished in his profuse praise on how well the public had taken to my work and how proud he was of me. "Victoria routinely hosts exhibits. I'm sure she'll have you come back. Next time consider including no less than ten paintings."

The following month Preston had come to town. It wasn't unusual that we made plans to meet up and go out to dinner. It was a humid July evening. The above the knee sundress I wore was more so to keep me cool. When Preston picked me up, I noticed his heated gaze for a split second, but didn't give it much thought. Boundaries had been established. Our relationship was platonic. Nothing more. Over dinner we chatted and laughed. I was insanely jealous of the flight Preston was taking the next evening to Madrid where his latest work was going to be on exhibit for the next three months.

"Take me with you," I had playfully pleaded, reaching across the table dramatically, grabbing his hands.

He had chuckled at my antics. "How fast can you pack?"

I brushed off his comment as pure teasing.

Like all the other times, Preston had seen me home safely. Except this time was different. He'd asked to come inside to use the bathroom before heading back to his hotel. I had no reason not to trust him. Or so I thought.

Once inside, what had been a pleasant evening with someone I had considered a mentor turned into a nightmare. It had taken less than fifteen minutes for Preston to violate me and change my life forever.

Seven

Motionless, Chanel stared at me, a storm brewing in the depth of her dark eyes. I knew my sister and could tell she wanted to tear some stuff up. Her gaze landed on a photo of Manny when he was a baby. The moment of realization struck her when she covered her mouth to muffle a sob.

"Ella, why didn't you tell me? All this time I thought..."

She thought what everyone in my family assumed. What I let them assume. That Preston and I had a summer fling that resulted in the conception of my son.

"I was too ashamed." I dashed away a tear. "I should've known better than to get close to Preston. That first time he kissed me I should've walked away and never looked back."

But I didn't walk away because regardless of his inappropriate behavior I was still enamored with Preston's talent as an artist. I trusted him when he said he was cool with us just being friends. Why else would he introduce me to one of Atlanta's prominent art gallery owners and fill my head with promises of helping me to exhibit my work in galleries all over

The States? I couldn't fathom what blindly trusting him would cost me.

Chantel's head shaking was vigorous. "No, Ella. This is on Preston! He took what he wanted when you told him all you wanted was friendship. That bastard knew what he was doing."

Dropping my head, the heels of my hands supported my forehead. My fingers sank into my curly afro. Six months after the incident, Preston called from a number I didn't recognize trying to do damage control. Yeah, six months later. "Ella, we both had too much to drink that night. We got carried away..."

"We? No, Preston! You got carried away and now I will never be rid of you!"

Days later, a persistent pounding on my door woke me from a deep slumber. Waddling to the door, I opened it to face my mortal enemy. Two combatants, we stared each other down. Preston never questioned or denied Manny's paternity. I wished he had. Instead, he used it as a weapon to control me.

A predator studied their prey. Defenses down, I had shared with Preston my feelings of inadequacy. And how I felt I had let my family, especially my grandparents, down. I didn't become a "real" artist. There was no way I was going to tell them I had been foolish enough to put myself in a vulnerable position. I should've been smarter and I wasn't. I didn't want to give them another reason to be disappointed in me.

Weak, I didn't have it in me to fight. Who would believe me? It wasn't like he was some random stranger who had snatched me off the streets. I had let him into my apartment. So, I never reported Preston to the authorities. Especially with him hinting at joint custody if I didn't allow him to see Manny whenever the mood struck him. Thank God the mood rarely did hit him.

A few months after Manny was born, Preston began

dating a well-known model. With his attention elsewhere, he didn't make any demands. But that didn't stop him from inserting himself in my life uninvited. Preston had his lawyer contact me to set up monthly deposits into my bank account to provide financial support for Manny. It must've been guilt eating at him. Whether it was or not, I didn't care. It only made me loathe him even more.

I lifted my head to gaze at my sister. "I also kept quiet because he said he would ruin me in the art community. To prove it, he told Victoria one of the paintings I had on exhibit was Ilona's."

An unchecked tear slid down my cheek. Furious, Victoria had called me cussing me out. She called me every bitch she could think of. "Do you know what would happen to my reputation if this ever got out?"

Stunned, I never got a word in to defend myself before she hung up on me. Weeks later, the painting she kept in her gallery was shipped to me. When I unwrapped it, it felt like someone had stabbed me in the chest. FRAUD was written across my work in bold red letters. Every now and then I looked at that ruined painting to remind me never to trust anyone else with my gift.

Chantel's lip curled in disgust. "I hate him. I really do."

I supposed Preston being Manny's father wouldn't allow me to hold that same sentiment. More so to protect my baby from any spillage of negativity that might pollute his innocence. Preston was a non-factor in my life. A necessary evil I had to put up with until Manny was of age.

"Don't waste your energy hating Preston. It's not going to change who he is."

"Ella, we need a game plan. This is going to be the last time he sends you an email like that."

"Like what? What can we do?"

"I don't know. We'll come up with something." Chantel paused for a second. "Are you going to tell Mom and Dad? Or Grandma Rose and Granddad X?"

The thought of telling my family the truth sent me in a panic. I jumped up and paced. My armpits became wet. "No, Chantel, I can't."

Always a challenger, Chantel jumped up too and stood in front of me. She placed her hands on my shoulders to keep me from moving. "Keeping silent is giving Preston power over you. He needs to know your family is behind you."

"Chantel, I can't."

"Yes, you can," she whispered, pulling me into an embrace.

My sister held me and I released tears of anger and sorrow until there was nothing else left. Unloading that horrific secret lifted a burden that had beat me into the ground. If I didn't have my son and my sister, I would've been buried years ago.

"Mommy, what's wrong?"

Manny's inquiry pulled me and Chantel apart. When she turned to face him, Manny's eyes lit up.

"Aunt Chantel!"

Chantel stooped down. Arms opened wide, she received Manny as he ran into them.

"Hey, baby!"

Manny giggled from Chantel peppering kisses all over his face. "I've missed you, little man."

"I missed you too, Aunt Chantel. Are we going on a trip?"

Chantel and I both laughed. My sister's arrival usually meant we were hopping on a plane heading somewhere.

"Not this time, Manny. Aunt Chantel came to visit for a few days."

Glancing up at me, her arms still around Manny, she said, "I think I'm going to stay longer than a few days."

Manny pumped his fist. "Yes! You can sleep in my bed and I can sleep in my sleeping bag."

"Aww, that's so sweet of you, Manny. Aunt Chantel can stay in the guestroom." My plan was to turn that room into my home studio. I'd rather give the room up to my sister.

A loud bang on the door startled us.

"You expecting anyone this early on a Saturday?"

It was eight-fifteen. I hadn't really connected with anyone since being back in Colemanville. Couldn't imagine who would be stopping by unannounced.

"Manny, go brush your teeth while I fix breakfast."

Oblivious to my anxiety, Manny took off running up the stairs. On my heels, Chantel followed me to the door.

A middle-aged man with red hair and freckles was on the other side of the door. His hand behind his back.

"Ella Caswell?"

"Yes."

He withdrew a legal size envelope from behind his back and shoved it at me. "You've been served."

"What the hell?" Chantel grumbled, snatching the envelope because I was too stunned. She slammed the door in the man's face and frantically ripped the envelope open. We read the legal document. I couldn't believe what I was reading. I reread several of the lines.

"Preston is suing me for joint custody."

Taking the document from my sister, I grabbed my laptop off the end table and headed for the stairs. "Please fix Manny's breakfast for me."

Inside my bedroom I closed the door and locked it before flopping down on my bed. My fingers swiftly glided over the keyboard as I opened up his email. While reading his email last night, I noticed a phone number at the bottom. Trembling, I dialed the number. I intentionally didn't block mine on the chance that Preston wouldn't answer a private number. A drowsy female voice answered on the fourth ring.

"Hello."

I recognized the voice.

"Let me speak to Preston." I didn't care about decorum or the woman in his bed.

"Excuse me? Who is this?"

"It's Ella, Victoria. Now put Preston on the phone."

"Ella! What are you doing calling—"

There was ruffling in the background. Victoria's voice sounded muffled as she questioned again why I was calling. I didn't give Preston a chance to take control of the conversation.

"Why do you want partial custody of my son?"

"You mean our son? It's time for him to be in my life on a regular basis."

This man woke up out of a dead sleep arrogant.

My heart felt like it was about to leap out of my chest. My hysteria rose, causing me to snap.

"Him has a name! And he's not your son. Emanuel is my son!"

Preston's chuckle was meant to taunt me. "What's with the dramatics, Ella? I've let you have your way for the last seven years. I want to see my son...*Emanuel*."

Full of venom, I struck fast and hard. "Are you prepared to tell Emanuel how he became your son...*Preston*? Because when the time is right, he will know the truth."

There was a long pause. I thought Preston had disconnected the call.

"Are you threatening me?"

The ominous tone of Preston's deep voice was meant to intimidate, but it only fueled me. Yes, my son's conception was under the most vile condition. Diagnosed with irregular periods in my twenties from the stress of a crazy travel schedule, I didn't think anything out of the ordinary when I didn't get my period for four months. I had made the choice to give my son life, unsure if I would be able to love him completely. My entire pregnancy I journaled every thought, every emotion. Poured out my fears to God. Lashed out my anger at God asking Him why He had allowed this to happen to me? What sin had I committed to deserve being violated? It was the social worker at the clinic where I was receiving my prenatal care who helped me to see that I hadn't done anything wrong. God wasn't punishing me for some unnamed sin I had committed. I never asked her if she was a Christian. I assumed she was when she reminded me of something I'd learned going to church as a child. "Ella, God loves you and He is with you." When my son was born and laid on my bare chest, we stared into each other's eyes. Until this day I didn't know if I was imagining it or not, but I heard a faint whisper. "God is with us." And that was how my son got the name Emanuel. It'd always been God, me, and Manny. So far God's protection had always covered me and my son. How had I forgotten that?

"No...I'm not threatening you. I don't know what your agenda is with all of a sudden wanting partial custody of Manny. I know how you move, Preston. I see how every other year you're engaged and then a few months later your messy break up is all over social media. You will not play with my son."

There was no denying Preston was talented and moved in social circles most artists would never have the opportunity to move in. Having access to those circles had allowed him to intermingle with famous and wealthy women he used to his advantage. Chantel was engrossed with keeping up with the latest gossip on celebrities. Every time one of his fiancées financed one of his projects, my sister was ringing my phone off the hook. My gut was telling me that somehow Preston needed Manny to be visible in his life. But why?

"I'll see you in court."

"Preston, watch where you step."

I didn't give him a chance to say another word. Disconnecting the call, I fell back on the bed and threw my forearm over my eyes. Chantel was right. I needed to talk to our parents. Before I did though, I needed to quiet my spirit. Pray. Be cleansed of Preston and his foolishness.

Eight

"Mommy? Let me in."

Manny knocking at the door startled me awake. It took several seconds for my head to rise off the pillow. I glanced over at the clock on the nightstand. Forty minutes had passed by after I hung up on Preston. Tormented by the ominous email, I hardly slept last night. Exhausted after my confrontation with Preston, I dozed off.

"Mommy?"

"Coming, Manny."

In his hand he held a plastic mason jar with a lid and straw containing what looked like a smoothie. "Aunt Chantel said to give this to you."

Instead of taking the jar, I kneeled before my son and nestled his head against my bosom. Manny's free arm wrapped around my waist. I inhaled the scent of his freshly washed hair from the night before. It pained me that someday I was going to have to shatter my baby's innocence with the truth.

"Mommy, why your heart sound funny?"

"Because I love you, Manny." Gently, I pulled his head

away from my bosom to stare into his eyes. "Mommy loves you so much."

I couldn't control the tears ready to spill over the brims of my eyes.

Manny leaned in and kissed my cheek. "I love you too, Mommy. Can I go to Grandma Rose and Granddad X house? Granddad X said he's going to take me to the dairy for ice cream."

Greedy little thing. My son's appetite has been hardy from the womb. He never missed an opportunity to eat anything, especially sweet treats.

Laughing, I tweaked his nose. Grateful that a wrecking ball hadn't yet destroyed his innocence. "It's may I go. Not can I go."

I took the jar from Manny and took a sip of its contents. "Mmmm, your auntie makes the best smoothies." It was a perfect blend of strawberry, pineapple, and banana with a hint of clover honey.

Opening his mouth like a baby bird, Manny took a sip of my smoothie. Silly as ever, he rubbed his tummy. "That's good, Mommy!"

When he went to take another sip, I snatched the jar away. "Un-uhn, go tell your auntie to make you one."

Manny made a funny face at me. "She already did."

"Boy! Get out of my room and get dressed while I call Grandma Rose and Granddad X. You better hurry up if you want to go to the dairy."

I cracked up when Manny went running down the hall to his room with his hands up in the air waving them from side to side. "I'm going!"

Chantel was coming out of the bathroom and almost collided with Manny. "Whoa, nephew! Slow down."

"I can't, Auntie. I'm going to the dairy for ice cream."

Manny slammed his door shut. He was the typical little

boy. He didn't care if he wore stripes with plaids. From the age of three he was fussy about dressing himself and picking out his own clothes. I learned to buy a wardrobe where just about all his clothing pieces were well coordinated. Sunday evenings I ironed Manny's clothes and hung his outfits in the closet. It made him feel like a big boy that he picked out what he wore every day. It wasn't going to take him long since he only had two outfits left. One for today and one for church tomorrow.

"You okay?"

Chantel sat down on the bed beside me and tried to take a sip of my smoothie. I moved the jar out of her reach. "I wish you and Manny would let me enjoy my smoothie in peace. And yes, now I'm okay. I was a little shaken up about getting served custody papers." I took a long sip of my drink. "I called him."

When Chantel reached for the jar, I handed it over. "What did you say to him?"

She listened as I replayed the conversation.

"He's a jackass. And I think you're right. He's up to something."

"But what? What could it be, Chantel?"

Frustrated, I let out a sigh. "I don't understand his sudden interest in Manny. Manny is seven...and Preston has seen him less than ten times his entire life. Something's not adding up."

"Yeah, I know. As Grandma Rose always says..."

We both repeated in unison, "It's gonna come out in the wash."

"You ready?"

I answered my sister honestly. I wasn't about to pretend I was at ease with exposing my trauma to our mother. "No, I'm not. Maybe we should've went to Dad's first."

After Chantel and I dropped Manny off at our grandparents we decided it would be best to talk to our mother first.

"It's going to be alright."

I gave my sister the side eye. "I'm not you, Chantel."

Mom seemed to be more compassionate where my sister was concerned. Although she got lectured, it was laced with tenderness. That consideration almost never came my way. I'd learned to live with it and not let it come between me and Chantel.

Chantel pouted. "It will be."

"Will it?"

I knew my mother loved me, but it seemed like I could never be exactly what she wanted me to be. Whenever the next opportunity presented itself, I didn't want her to throw up in my face that if I had returned to Colemanville to work with her this nightmare with Preston would have never happened to me. Rosaline Caswell had her way of telling you "I told you so" without coming out directly and saying it. Part of me wanted to turn around. But the other part of me knew it was time for me to do what my therapist had encouraged me to do years ago.

"Ella, this is serious. Give Mom the benefit of the doubt," Chantel pleaded.

Letting out a doubtful breath, I opened the car door. "Let's go."

As we made our way from the car to the front door of our childhood home, I whispered a prayer that my mother would show me grace. My soul couldn't take a fraction of callousness.

Standing shoulder to shoulder with Chantel, I rang the doorbell. We waited several minutes for Mom to answer. Her car was parked in the driveway, indicating she was home. If she had gone out of town, my grandparents would have mentioned it.

Chantel knocked on the door and still no answer.

Worried, I turned to Chantel. "You think we should go in?"

"Yeah, it's not like Mom not to answer. You think she still keeps a key in the hiding place?"

"Probably. I'll be right back."

It didn't take me long to go around to the back of the house and get the key Mom kept hidden under a loose brick in the backyard walkway. When Chantel and I entered the house, nothing looked out of order. I didn't smell anything that could've been a decomposing body which calmed my nerves. *Girl, you watch too much crime television.*

"You look down here. I'll go upstairs."

At the top of the stairs, I cocked my head to the side when I heard feminine, playful laughter. *Mom?*

"Woman, when are you going to let me come back home?" *Dad?*

"Never. I love sneaking around with you, Owen. Reminds me of when we were kids. Lifting up the kitchen window for you to climb in after Mama and Daddy had gone to bed."

Dad's chuckle was deep and dare I admit...sexy? *Yuck!*

"Love, I'm too old to climb through windows."

Whaaat?

My movement in the hallway caused one of the wooden floor planks to squeak.

"Who's out there?"

Chantel was coming up the stairs. I put my finger to my lips to hush her. I mouthed, "Dad is here."

I had to slap my hand over my mouth to keep from laughing out loud from the way Chantel's eyebrows shot up.

"With Mom?" she mouthed back.

"I said who's out there?" Mom's tone was frantic as if caught doing something she had no business doing.

Dad peeked his head out the door dressed in his navy

bathrobe. His eyes lit up and a huge grin spread across his handsome face. "Hey! What are you two doing here?"

"Ella and Chantel?"

We giggled like we were kids again. "Yes, Mom," we called out.

Dad hugged me first then Chantel before moving aside to allow us into the bedroom they were obviously sharing again.

It was eleven thirty in the morning and Mom had some serious postcoital hair she was trying to smooth down. Face flushed, she had the white bedsheet pulled up to her chest and snugly tucked underneath her arms.

"Is something wrong with Mama or Daddy?" Alarmed, her hand flew to her chest. "Is it Manny? Chantel, when did you come home?"

"No, Mom. They're okay and Manny is with them. Chantel came home..." I reached out and my sister took my hand. "Because I needed her."

Dad came over to me and tilted my head up so he could look me in the eyes. "What's going on, baby doll?"

Chantel gently squeezed my hand letting me know I was doing the right thing.

"We'll go downstairs and wait for you and Mom to get dressed."

Chantel and I went into the kitchen to raid Mom's refrigerator. As sisters we had a lot in common. Stress eating was one of them. We spoke in hushed tones of how I was going to start the discussion over slices of ham, brie, and gourmet crackers.

Thirty minutes later, our parents emerged freshly showered from their late morning tryst. Ever the southern lady, Mom's hair was pulled back in a low bun. I couldn't tell if the glow was from her strict skincare regimen and lightly applied makeup making her appear younger. Or her rekindled love affair with Dad. Looking my Dad over, I noticed he had shed a few pounds.

"That bad, huh?" Mom sat beside me at the massive kitchen island, taking a cracker and dipping it in the soft cheese.

I almost choked on the piece of ham I was swallowing. It was beyond bad.

Before I could answer, Dad chimed in as he took the seat beside Chantel. "Do I have to pull out my boxing gloves?"

Dad had joined the Navy at seventeen after graduating high school for the G.I. Bill to put him through college. During his four years of active service and four years in the reserves, he took up boxing to stay busy and out of trouble. He was pretty good at it and could've gone pro if he and Mom hadn't married after she graduated high school.

Mom clucked her tongue. "Owen, don't be so barbaric. Ella baby, what's going on?"

My eyes grew misty from the childhood endearment my mom used to call me before I reached puberty and developed a mind of my own, challenging her on almost everything. I twisted the napkin in my hand into tiny pieces. Head hung low, I couldn't look at either one of my parents. I closed my eyes because this was the only way I was going to get out what I had come here for. When the first word left my lips, I didn't stop. I didn't stop at the first tear splash hitting the back of my hand resting on my lap. I didn't stop at the sound of the gut-wrenching sobs coming from my mother. And I didn't stop at the explosive expletives my father shouted swearing to rip Preston's throat out.

Inhaling, I lifted my head and exhaled as I opened my eyes. I was convinced there was something sacred about a mother's bosom. Just as I had done hours earlier with Manny, my mother drew me to her, rested my head in her bosom, and held me. Her body trembled. I could feel her tears saturating my hair, cleansing me.

"Ella baby, I'm sorry. I'm so sorry. I should've been there for you."

"You're here now, Mom."

She framed my face in her soft hands. "Don't you worry. That horrible man will not get his hands on Manny. I promise you that. Isn't that right, Owen?"

"Yes, love. Ella, your mother and I will not let anything happen to you or our grandson."

Dad and Chantel wrapped their arms around us too. I had never felt so loved in all my life. Suddenly, my thirty-nine years didn't feel so grown. And that was okay with me. I'd been carrying this burden for way too long by myself. I could breathe a little easier with the support of my family.

"I'm moving back to Colemanville, too."

I wiggled out of the snug cocoon to gaze at my sister. "Chantel, you don't have to do that."

"Stop telling me what I don't have to do. I'm not going to be miles away from you and Manny with that egomaniac on the loose. My lease is up in three months, but I know someone who's willing to sublet it until then. You know I'm not attached to any one place."

Yeah, I did know because I was the same way. Things were changing though. I wanted stability for Manny. Stability for me.

"Besides, you're going to be busy with getting your studio and gallery up and running. You're going to need someone to watch Manny."

Dad commented, "Chantel is right, Ella. We're all going to have to make sure eyes are always on Manny."

Mom perked up. "Manny can tag along with me to the office." She shrugged. "Who knows...maybe my grandson will be my successor."

"Or maybe mine," Dad piped in, causing my mother to huff.

"Owen—"

I made the timeout sign with my hands. Personally, I didn't see my son being in real estate or accounting. "Manny says he wants to be a clown so he can make people laugh."

Dad and Chantel cracked up. Mom rolled her eyes and grumbled, "Oh, dear God."

I couldn't help laughing at my mother. "Mom, I'm teasing. The only thing Manny wants to be now is a little boy playing with his toys and taste tester for Grandma Rose's cakes, cookies, and pies."

Mom pinched my cheek. "And so he shall be."

Chantel and I shared a look. All wasn't well. But it was on its way to being so.

Nine

"Who is that fine specimen who keeps looking over here at you?"

"Shhh, I'm trying to listen to the sermon."

Discreetly, I looked around to make sure no one had heard my sister. Chantel wasn't one for decorum when she wanted to be nosy. Like now on a Sunday morning during church service. I didn't need her asking me about the *fine specimen* who pulled up in the shiny red vintage Mustang as Manny and I were headed up the stairs into the sanctuary of Evergreen Missionary Baptist Church. Before Manny could get to waving, I grabbed him by the hand and ushered him to the lower level where the children attended Children's Church. By the time I hurried upstairs, Chantel had taken a seat in the pew across the aisle from where the Mustang's owner was sitting.

I tried hard not to keep my gaze from wandering to him. But my eyeballs wouldn't obey me. His profile showcased a strong aquiline nose, high cheekbones, and a chiseled jawline. In a split second, with the slight turn of his head, our gazes connected and held for a moment. The barely there smile on his full lips made my stomach flutter.

"Somebody's feeling you," Chantel sang under her breath.

The rush of heat rising up my neck wasn't from a hot flash. I had at least another eight to ten years before I would be sitting somewhere breaking out in a sweat and fanning myself. When was the last time I blushed? Eons ago. Being a single mother nor having time for relationships wasn't likely the reason my body lacked an automatic response like blushing. My trust had been abused. Ruined by the opposite sex. I didn't hate men. I was just wary of the ones I didn't know. My grandfather, father, uncles, cousins, and the decent men I grew up around in Colemanville were the reason I didn't believe all men were inherently evil.

"Ow, why'd you do that?"

"Keep talking while I'm trying to listen to the sermon and I'mma pinch you again."

Chantel crossed her arms and stared straight ahead, leaving me alone for the rest of the service. After the benediction, I hightailed it over to see Nana Flo. Although she and her family belonged to First Jubilee AME Church, from time to time, they visited Evergreen and our family would visit Jubilee.

Since I'd moved back to Colemanville, I hadn't had time to make my way out to Sims Stables to visit with her. I knew I needed to do better. In Colemanville, growing up, not only did our parents raise and influence us, so did our neighbors. Particularly the elders of the community. Young girls looked up to Nana Flo as someone they wanted to emulate. She wore many hats—wife, mother, business owner, community leader —and seemed to do it effortlessly with grace.

Gifted with a Kodak camera by my grandparents at my sweet sixteen party, I was on a mission to snap shots of any and everything. Nana Flo gave me my first photography gig. Twice a month, on Saturday morning at seven-thirty sharp, I was at the shop to take photos of hair models. Back then I wasn't skilled at coaxing out every day women's inner supermodel. Never one to crush a dream, Nana Flo kept every photo. Even the bad ones. The exceptionally good ones she hung in the shop. The others were relegated to a large black portfolio she kept in the waiting area. I was immensely proud of my work. How could I not be when Grandma Rose bragged to the entire town that I was the photographer who'd taken the shots of the models lining the walls of Iva's House of Beauty.

"There's my little photographer. Come give Nana Flo some sugah."

I had to stoop down in my heels to give the town's matriarch a kiss on the cheek and a hug. A flood of warm memories washed over me of sleepovers with Jillian and Kristen at the Sims estate, staying up into the wee hours of the morning giggling and playing with dolls, rushed through me. Later, as we grew older, gossiping and talking about boys replaced the dolls. Papa Packer gave us riding lessons and Nana Flo tolerated us underfoot in the kitchen as she prepared meals.

"I'm sorry I haven't been to the ranch to see you, Nana Flo."

Gently, Nana Flo held me away from her. "Now hush up all that apologizing. I know you would've eventually stopped by to see about me. How long are you in town for?"

My eyes grew misty. I should've come back to Colemanville years ago. "I'm home to stay, ma'am."

Those blue-gray eyes of Nana Flo's lit up. "Praise Jesus! I'm trying to talk Jillian into coming down with the kids for the Juneteenth celebration. Maybe stay a while."

Before I could comment on Jillian's potential visit, Nana Flo glided onto something else. "What are you going to do in Colemanville?" Nana Flo's question wasn't an unusual one. Another one of her teachings was that women needed to be self-governing in chartering their own path in life.

I hadn't seen Mom and Grandma Rose ease up beside me.

"She's going to open up a photography studio and art gallery," Grandma Rose chimed in. She looped her arm through mine, her head held high in a regal fashion. I was grateful for the pride in her voice fortifying my self-confidence.

"Is that right?"

"Yes, ma'am. The studio is going to be where the old catering hall used to be."

"Over there on Beacon Lane? Near my old shop?"

I nodded. "Yes, ma'am."

"That's a good thing. We don't need no riff raff setting up mischief downtown."

Several blocks over from Beacon Lane, a northerner had moved to town and opened a nightclub masquerading as a catering hall to meet the zoning requirements. The problem wasn't that an outsider had opened a business. The problem was the clientele from neighboring towns that had been drawn to Colemanville with their rowdy behavior disturbing the peace of the locals. There were rumors of unlawful activities going on in the establishment. That didn't go over well with the community. Residents of Colemanville had banded together and marched down to city hall to demand something be done. Granddad X said in less than a year the business was shut down and the owner left town.

"Amen to that, Miss Flo. Our town ain't used to no foolishness," my grandmother commented, tilting her head toward the town's matriarch.

"Speaking of the catering hall... Ella, I want to introduce you to the young man who owns the rubbish removal business," my mother interrupted. Once Grandma Rose and Nana Flo got to going on about preserving the town, we'd be liable to be standing here until dinner time.

Mom leaned over me to kiss Nana Flo on the cheek. "How are you, Nana Flo?"

"Pretty good, Rosaline. Will I see you at the DOLLs fundraiser next week?"

"I will be there. Bright and early."

Nana Flo grinned at my mother. "Are you going to bring those gourmet donuts you get from over in Jacksonville?"

Mom threw her head back and laughed when Grandma Rose gave Nana Flo the side eye. If I had to guess, my grandmother was calling her friend a traitor for requesting the donuts when she was the finest baker in all of North Carolina.

"Yes, ma'am. I'll bring the donuts." Mom turned to my grandmother. "Mama, Owen and I will meet you and Daddy outside."

"Alrighty. I'll be out shortly. I want to talk to Miss Flo for a few minutes."

We said our goodbyes to Nana Flo. Mom held my hand, which any other time would have felt awkward, almost unnatural. After I purged my secret, Mom and I took a stroll through the neighborhood. We ended up on a park bench in front of the library. For the first time I was able to express my deepest feelings without fear of retribution. Somewhere around the age of twelve, a passion for painting and photography took root inside of me. In the beginning Mom would do what was expected of any mother. Praise me for winning art contests and proudly display my certificates and ribbons on the mantle. The contention between us began to fester when I applied to universities with art and photography majors. Mom wanted me to go to business school, then get a real estate license. As a kid, on the rare occasions when she couldn't find a babysitter for me and Chantel, we were forced to tag along to open houses. And I hated it. Nothing about selling someone their dream home or commercial property fed my creative soul.

I hadn't forgotten her harsh words meant to deter me, but instead bruised my spirit. "You'll never be as talented as Grandmother."

On that bench, I made her aware of how her words had crushed me.

It did matter that everyone else praised my work and told me I was extremely talented. I relished in the praise. Yet, there was still a longing to have my mother acknowledge my work. Just to be a *little* bit proud of me. I never blamed my mother for what happened to me. But late at night, all alone when the world was quiet, I would lie in bed and wonder if I had had my mom's approval would I have been blinded by Preston's admiration of my work?

To my mother's credit, she listened and for once hadn't become defensive. Her apology was sincere. It moved me to tears.

"I will do better as a mother. I'm sorry I haven't supported you like I should. But that doesn't mean I'm not going to have *my* opinions. You're still my child at almost forty and I've earned the right to have a say so...sometimes."

Mom had paused to dab at the tear rolling out of the corner of her eye. "I do love you, Ella. I never meant to hurt you. I only wanted what I thought was best for you."

"How're you feeling? Did you sleep well?"

Mom's query drew me out of my musing.

"Feel better now that you and Dad know everything. Hardly slept at all. Chantel and I were up most of the night talking."

I held my breath praying she didn't ask what we talked about. After we digested our parents' reaction to my past and present history with Preston and the heartfelt talk Mom and I had, the conversation landed on our folks' rekindled love affair. From what little bit I overheard in the hallway, it sounded like they'd been an item again for some time. Chantel predicted they would be remarried by the end of the year. I didn't agree. Mom sounded like she was content with her and Dad's clandestine rendezvous.

"Thank you for trusting me and your father with such a delicate matter."

I didn't have time to respond as we continued to make our way toward the back of the sanctuary. Manny was charging toward me with a piece of brown construction paper cut out in the shape of a boat.

"Mommy, Grandmom, look! We learned about Noah's ark. Two of every kind of animal was on the boat. And it rained for forty days and forty nights. That's a long time!"

Mom and I shared a smile. My parents schemed up a plan to take turns globe hopping with Manny before they'd let Preston get partial custody of their grandchild. It was Chantel who reminded them they would be kidnappers and hunted down by the FBI that caused them to ditch that plan.

"Let me see that," Mom said, reaching for Manny's artwork. With her free hand she took Manny's hand as we exited the church.

"This is beautiful. Do you think you can make me one to put on my mantle?"

Instead of answering my mother, Manny pointed excitedly. "Mommy, there's the nice man with the red car."

"Ah, isn't this interesting?" Mom's mauve matte-colored lips curved in a smile.

The flutters in my stomach kicked up again. Fine specimen was headed in our direction. "Isn't what interesting?" I whispered behind a smile.

"Good afternoon, Ms. Caswell. You're looking beautiful as always."

I had to give my mom the side eye. She had the nerve to be blushing *and* grinning. I couldn't blame her though. Who wouldn't be with a handsome man complimenting your looks.

Mom batted her eyes. "Why thank you, Hassan." She turned to me and winked. I wanted to crawl into the crack on the sidewalk.

"Hassan Murphy, this is my daughter, Ella Caswell. I've told you about her. She'll be setting up her photography studio and art gallery in the old catering hall over on Beacon Lane."

Hassan. I love that name. It fits him.

The corner of Hassan's mouth curled in a smile, causing my knees to go weak.

"We've met...sort of."

We hadn't exchanged names.

Hassan held his hand out. When I placed mine in his, calluses grazed the soft skin on my palm.

"Nice to see you again, Ella."

"Same here, Hassan."

Hassan released my hand to stoop down in front of Manny. He stuck his hand out for my son to shake. "Hi, Manny. How's it going?"

"Good, Mr. Hassan. Did you drive your car?"

"I sure did. It's right down the street."

"Can I go for a ride in your car?"

Before I could tell Manny that would be a resounding no, Hassan replied, "Only if it's okay with your mother."

Mom must've sensed my uneasiness. Thankfully she guided the conversation back to why she was introducing us.

"Hassan, dear, I told Ella your company would do a great job at clearing out the building."

"What timeline are you looking at to open?"

Yesterday, I wanted to answer. Just last week I received appointments for engagement and maternity photoshoots in Jacksonville. Both parties were fine with doing the shoots outdoors at local historical sites. It would've been ideal to have my studio open and operational as an alternative if the weather didn't cooperate.

"If possible, I'd like to be open for business by fall." Another busy time of the year for family holiday photo shoots.

Hassan reached into his back pocket to retrieve a silver clip that held money and business cards. He handed me a card with his name as the owner, phone number, and website.

"Sustainable Junk Pros." I glanced up from the card to gaze at him. "You're into recycling?"

Nodding, he confirmed, "I salvage as much as I can to be reused and kept out of landfills."

I tapped the card against the palm of my hand. The thin gold bracelets I wore clinked against each other. When his gaze followed my movement, I wished I'd kept up with manicures. Although that sort of pampering wasn't practical in my line of work.

"I love that. It's not fair to my son's generation and following generations to potentially be left with a dying planet from unnecessary waste."

Dramatically, Hassan put his hand to his wide chest. "Miss Ella, you're speaking my love language."

Mom and I laughed. I loved that he called me Miss. I found that charming seeing as though Hassan didn't have a southern accent. Therefore, I couldn't label him as what Grandma Rose would call a true southern gentleman.

Like clockwork the ice cream truck could be heard in the distance. Toddlers and school aged little ones tugged at adults, pleading for an early afternoon treat. Manny was no different, turning those big, beautiful eyes on his grandmother. He knew better than to look at me.

"Come on, Manny."

Before I could object because the family was headed over to my grandparents for lunch, Mom intervened on Manny's behalf.

"I'll get him just a little something," she emphasized, holding up her hand, bringing her thumb and pointer finger together, barely touching.

Slightly annoyed, I mumbled, "Okay, Mom."

When she was out of hearing range, Hassan leaned in, lowering his voice. "It's a grandparent thing. We wouldn't understand."

I had to bite the inside of my cheek to keep from moaning. Hassan's deep voice was making me remember I was a woman. Especially with the way he was looking at me. His roaming gaze held masculine interest. Oddly enough I didn't feel uncomfortable. There was something almost reverent about it. I don't know. Maybe because we were standing on hallowed ground.

"You have children?"

Hassan's handsome face lit up at the mention of children. That simple reaction made me like him more than I would allow myself to admit and dissect for now.

"Two girls. Thirteen and eleven." His smile dimmed a bit. "I don't see them as often as I'd like."

I didn't know what to say to that last part. Sounded to me like there was some drama there that I wasn't about to hint at having any interest in knowing about. I had my own problems with Preston I had to navigate through and solve. So I did what I always did. I was going to run.

Ten

Of course, I couldn't make my getaway with Manny being fixated on Hassan's Mustang. Popsicle in hand, Manny ran over, leaving Mom behind talking to Ms. Smith, the Children's Church teacher.

"Mommy, can I ride in Mr. Hassan's car?"

Before I could form an excuse to gently let my son down, a colorful blur stole my words.

Chantel shimmed over in a hot pink pencil skirt, a white fitted blouse with capped sleeves, and four-inch pink heels she'd confiscated from my closet. Notes of her delicate perfume seductively permeated the air. Every male gaze was on my beautiful sister. I knew it was horrible of me to wish Hassan's eyes would glaze over in lust too. It would give me all I needed to squash those schoolgirl crush feelings I was having and had no idea what to do with.

Too bad Chantel hadn't come within pinching distance. From the smirk playing on her lightly pink glossed lips, Chantel was about to morph back into that nuisance of a younger sister, getting on my last nerve.

"Ella, aren't you going to introduce me to your friend?"

Oh, how I want to pinch her!

I smiled at Hassan, wondering why he wasn't smitten yet.

"Hassan, this is my sister Chantel" I turned to Chantel and gave her the evil eye. "Chantel, this is Hassan Murphy."

Hassan's smile was pleasant enough when he quickly shook Chantel's hand.

"Nice to meet you, Chantel."

Silly Chantel wiggled her eyebrows at me. A gesture we did when a guy was exceptionally handsome. "Likewise, Hassan."

Impatient, Manny tugged on my arm, all while munching on his popsicle. In the late May heat, orange liquid ran down his arm.

"Mommy?"

I shook my head, digging in my purse for a tissue. "No, Manny. Look..." I nodded my head to his arm. "You have popsicle juice running down your arm."

Dabbing at the stickiness with the last of my tissues, I tried to be firm. Manny was giving me that sad puppy dog look that always got him his way until I had enough of his shenanigans. Under Hassan's intense stare, I could only concentrate on one thing.

I broke it to Manny gently. "I don't want you making a mess in Mr. Hassan's car."

"Nothing that can't be cleaned up," Hassan piped in, giving Manny hope by the sudden gleam in my son's eyes.

Was this gang up on Ella day? I didn't like these odds. Three against one.

Chantel butted her pierced nose into my parental decision making.

"Give that to me, baby."

Without hesitation, Manny handed over the half-eaten treat. Chantel shimmied over to a nearby trashcan to dispose of it, causing good Christian men to sin. Their roaming gazes were covertly glued to her swaying hips. When we got home, I was gonna tell her not to wear that outfit to church again.

One would've thought Chantel had five kids hanging off of her the way she swooped down into her purse and pulled out a pack of wet wipes.

Hassan looked on, amused. Chantel took all of three seconds to wipe down Manny's sticky face, arm, and hands. "See, no messy Manny."

Holding up his hands, Manny's grin was adorable with his two front teeth halfway grown in. "I'm all clean, Mommy."

Defeated, I took my son's hand. "Let's go." What harm could come of taking a Sunday afternoon ride in a classic convertible?

THE BREEZE BLOWING through my curly hair felt good against my scalp. Hassan played smooth jazz as we cruised through downtown Colemanville, over to Copper Lake, and then on to the countryside. Manny was uncharacteristically quiet. I turned in my seat to glance back at him. Matchbox car clutched in his hand, he'd fallen asleep.

"I don't believe that boy. He harassed me to go for a ride and now he's back there sleeping."

Hassan chuckled. "Come on now, Mom. He wasn't harassing you. More like a fascination of riding in a real-life toy car."

"Yeah, who doesn't like a classic Mustang?" Mischief seeped out of me. An impish smirk twitched at the corners of my mouth. I checked the side mirror again to make sure Manny was still asleep. At ease with Hassan, I shared a story from my past.

"When I was a teenager me and my friends stole a Mustang just like this one."

It was a good thing we were on a dirt road with no cars around. Hassan had taken his eyes off the road to stare at me.

"You're kidding...right?"

I bit my bottom lip and shook my head. "Nope...well...we didn't exactly steal it."

Hassan chuckled again. "Not exactly? What does that mean?"

Like a devious kid, I dropped my head to conceal my grin. "We borrowed the car. It's different."

Hassan's eyebrows shot up. "Borrowed...interesting word choice. Please explain."

The entire time I was telling Hassan about how me, Kristin, and Jillian took the car from Mr. Harvey Jr's car shop to go joyriding, got arrested, and spent the night in jail, Hassan's hearty laughter did something to my soul. He had a contagious kind of laugh. I found myself laughing too.

"I would've never guessed you were a hellion."

The gold bangles on my wrist made music when I leaned my arm on the rolled down window. Something whimsical came over me as I smiled and remembered a time when I carelessly took risks. Even if it meant facing consequences later.

"No...not a hellion. More like an explorer." I laughed when I admitted, "Mixed with a drop of mischief."

Hassan laughed again. "How did Uncle Matt take you and your friends *borrowing* his prized possession?

"Wait a minute... Mr. Harvey Jr. is your uncle? How?"

Hassan pulled the vehicle to the side of the road bordering the Sims' estate. Plush green pastures and cows grazing in the distance were visible as far as the eye could see. I was tempted to wake up Manny, but decided against it. Outside of my sister, I hadn't had much conversation with an adult. I was going to take this time to engage the woman in me. Soon enough I'd be back to full mommy duties.

"He and my grandfather were half-brothers. Same mother, different fathers."

Interesting. I didn't recall Mr. Harvey Jr. having a brother. All I knew was that he was the son of Mr. Harvey, the original owner of the automotive repair shop. And had a sister, Ms. Elaine, who was the town's seamstress before moving away to live with her daughter in Virginia after her husband passed away.

"In a small town you know just about everybody's business. I never knew Mr. Harvey Jr. had a brother."

"Out of sight, out of mind. He left Colemanville the day he turned eighteen and went up north. The only time he ever came back was to attend their mother's funeral."

Before my mind could draw up scenarios of what caused Hassan's grandfather to leave and never come back, Hassan freely disclosed his grandfather's story.

"My grandfather had a rebellious streak. Didn't like structure or rules so he moved up north. Got caught up in some trouble in New Jersey and almost ended up going to jail. It was enough to scare him straight. He got a job as a sanitation worker, met and married my grandmother. Raised a family while going to college at night to get a degree in criminal justice. Granddad was a probation officer in juvenile court. Didn't pay a lot. That didn't matter to him. He was committed to helping teen boys in our community get back on the straight and narrow."

"I love that. Sometimes, I worry about Manny..."

I let my words trail off. I didn't know Hassan well enough to divulge my fears of my son not having a father in his life. How I worried that as a woman I would never be able to give him those special teachings that required a man's instructions.

"As long as you surround Manny with men who're willing to nurture him, he'll be fine."

"I hope so," I murmured. Preston's nonsense rushed to the front of my mind. *He's not getting my son.*

"Have faith, Ella. Ready to head back?"

I glanced over my shoulder at Manny and sent up a prayer for my child's protection. At this point faith was all I had.

"Yeah, I'm ready."

"How'd the drive go?"

I cut my eyes at Chantel, tempted to elbow her so she'd wobble into the street on her heels as we walked back home. Probably would've done it if Manny wasn't twenty steps ahead of us.

Recharged after his nap, Manny was going to be a handful to get to bed at his eight-thirty bedtime. Although school was out for summer break, I made it a habit to keep him on a routine schedule. Bathed and teeth brushed by seven-thirty. Thirty minutes of reading and then lights out.

"None of your business."

My sister knew I was messing with her by my exaggerated pout. I'd only seen Hassan twice and he was kicking up dust in my life, causing me to examine stuff I didn't want to consider exploring.

When he dropped me off at my grandparents', Manny wouldn't budge when I called his name. Before I could shake him awake, Hassan insisted on carrying Manny into my grandparents' home.

"Ella, show Hassan to the guest room to lay that baby down. No use in waking him up. Don't want to stunt that baby's growth," Grandma Rose had instructed. The gleam in her dark, wise eyes held curiosity as her gaze raked over Hassan carrying Manny as he slept.

Inwardly, I groaned at Grandma Rose's old wives' tale that possibly held a grain of truth to it. I wanted to insist that

Manny could've been taken to her and Granddad X's bedroom that was previously the den located on the first floor. Or simply wake him up.

The entire time I ascended the stairs I wanted to glance over my shoulder at Hassan carrying Manny. But I stopped myself from doing so. All it would've done was dredge up the surface fantasies I'd held in my heart of Manny having a loving father.

On the ride home I learned his daughters' names were Zuri and Kali. When Hassan spoke of his girls, the love and admiration in his voice was unmistakable. It was shameful to be jealous of children, but for a moment I was because my sweet Manny had never had that, would never have that. At least not from Preston. Preston's interactions with Manny always seemed forced. Calculated, even. The few times he held or hugged our son left Preston frustrated by Manny's reaction. Hearing my baby scream worse than getting a shot at his pediatric appointment sent me into mama bear mode, extricating Manny from Preston's clutches.

Hassan had gently laid Manny on the bed. He took a step back to gaze at him for several seconds. For those few moments, I pretended Manny had what would never be, a loving father.

When Manny had awakened from his nap, he searched the dining room where the family was gathered at the table chatting. He didn't ask to be fed or what treats Grandma Rose had baked.

"Where's Mr. Hassan?" Manny had dug into his pockets to withdraw a toy car from each. "I want to show him my cars."

His downfallen countenance shook me to my core. In no time Manny's love of cars was enough to forge a bond with Hassan. All I could do was make a promise I intended to keep.

"You can show Mr. Hassan your cars the next time we see him."

Because there would be a next time. If only for the sake of my son.

Chantel looped her arm through mine. "My dear sister... you are my business."

"That, I am."

I let out a soft sigh, remembering how carefree I felt in such close proximity to Hassan. Being literally two feet away from him hadn't freaked me out. His easy going presence melted away the awkwardness that left me feeling exposed.

Manny came to a halt at the stop sign, waiting for us to catch up with him. Like most small southern towns on a Sunday, traffic was almost nonexistent. Regardless, I checked for any moving vehicles before giving Manny the go ahead to cross to the other side of the street. I waited for Manny to get a few feet ahead.

"The ride was nice..." My cheeks grew warm. "Hassan *is* nice."

"That he is. He likes you."

I wanted to refute Chantel's observation. But I was way past the age of being coy and playing games.

"I know he does."

"What are you going to do about it?"

Good question. Did I want to do anything about it?

"Don't know."

"Are you at least open to getting to know him?"

"Maybe." Was about all I was willing to commit to for now.

Chantel grinned at me. "Maybe is good."

Eleven

"Tilt your head slightly to the right...yes, just like that..." I instructed the bride-to-be.

A natural beauty, her melanated skin glistened under the early morning July sun. The way the groom-to-be gazed longingly into his future wife's eyes would make anyone believe in love.

Copper Lake made a beautiful backdrop for the engagement photoshoot. The couple was agreeable to the location as they were raised in Colemanville. After college they moved away to Charlotte, North Carolina for work. They had expressed wanting their lifelong memories to be captured where their roots originated.

Whenever I took on a client, my services included a comprehensive intake interview. Any potential client who was opposed to participating, I didn't waste my time taking their business. Especially after I would explain the interview was for me to get to know them so I'd have the necessary information to make the photoshoot a memorable experience.

If every couple were like Audrey and Kwami, I'd be tempted to do only engagement photoshoots. Their youthful optimism of love was inspiring even to someone like me who gave up on falling in love years ago. I couldn't help being overcome with giddiness when learning they'd had a crush on each other in the fifth grade. Kwami was described by Audrey as, "a scrawny little thing." Their romance didn't blossom until Kwami got up the nerve to ask Audrey to junior prom. By then he was six-one and fine as hell according to the bride-to-be.

I supposed another reason the couple was endearing was because falling in love so young mirrored that of my parents' and grandparents' romances. The running joke in the family was that Chantel and I took after our great-grandmother, Ilona. According to my granddad's sister, Aunt Jessica, their mother Ilona had no desire to marry her first husband or birth his children. Ilona was decades ahead of her time, preferring to pursue her art over domestic life. I often wondered what Ilona would think of me and Chantel? Here I was, a single mother and small business owner on the verge of turning forty in December with no man. Chantel was in her mid-thirties, single with no children. Sometimes, I blamed myself for my sister's lackluster love life. How could she have one when she's never, not once, failed to drop whatever she had going on in her life to be there for me and Manny?

"You alright, Ella?"

Audrey's question snapped my wandering thoughts back to the present. "I'm good. Y'all ready to head over to the high school?"

Kwami wrapped his arm around Audrey's shoulder. "Yep, meet you over there."

As I gathered up my equipment, I watched the couple. Before my smile could take full form, my phone buzzed in my back pocket, signaling an incoming text.

See you in court next month.

Preston had taken to sending texts at least once a week

designed to rattle me. For the most part I ignored them because I knew I would *never* allow Manny to be unsupervised with Preston. When I did respond it was to tell him to go to hell. Today though, his taunting hit a nerve.

Let's see what the judge thinks when he/she learns my son is the result of rape.

I pressed the heel of my hands to the corners of my eyes to keep the tears from falling. I despised Preston for torturing me with the thought of having to share my son with him. Loathed him for thinking he could excuse his sexual assault by providing financially for Manny. Mom and Chantel had comforted me when I expressed regret over being agreeable to Preston setting up a legal agreement to provide for Manny until he was eighteen. At the time I was consumed with navigating the ins and outs of being a mother to a newborn I hadn't planned on having and making up lies to cover my lack of common sense when it came to believing all Preston had wanted was friendship and to mentor me. I detested Preston even more, as of late, for the constant reminder of how my sweet Manny had come to be. When Preston wasn't hovering like some damn evil hawk, I didn't think of that sickening summer night. All my heart allowed me to grasp was the unconditional love it held for Emanuel. Because through it all, God was with us.

That thought grounded me. As well as the attorney, Silas Goode, I'd consulted with after getting over the shock of Preston being serious about going after partial custody. I'd known Silas my entire life. He was a few years younger than me and was sweet on Chantel when we were growing up. His family law practice served the Colemanville, Jacksonville, and Fayetteville areas. It was humiliating to have to divulge my past with Preston, but necessary. This was one fight I was going to be prepared for.

I finished packing up my equipment and headed to the

high school. My day was too busy to get weighed down with Preston's bullying tactics. After the shoot, I was headed over to the studio. Hassan and his two-man crew had completed cleaning out the former catering hall. Later, I promised I would take Manny and Noah to Copper Lake to ride their bikes. Several years ago, the city council had approved the installation of a bike path around the lake.

As I headed to my car, my cell rang again. *This better not be that fool again.*

"Hello Ella, it's Hassan. Can you stop by today?"

"I was planning on it after I finished the photoshoot. Everything okay?"

I held my breath. I wasn't in the mood for any bad news. *Lord please don't let there be any busted pipes or foundation issues.*

"You'll see when you get here."

From the easy flow of Hassan's words coated in his rich baritone, I blew out a relieved sigh.

"Okay, good..."

"You good?"

I didn't know why, but those two simple words calmed my spirit, making my soul smile. "Yep. See you soon."

WHEN I WALKED UP to the gallery, Hassan and two other workers were inside taking sledgehammers to a plaster wall. Hassan's locs were pulled back in a ponytail. The black tank style shirt he had on was littered with white particles of plaster. In this heat he wore Levi's jeans riding low on his hips. Timberland boots protected his feet. Out of his back pocket hung a navy bandana.

Blindly, I reached into my leather tote for my Nikon Z8. Placing my bag on the ground in front of me, I positioned myself at an angle so I could capture Hassan's profile. I snapped shots of him swinging the sledgehammer, decimating the wall. With each swing his biceps and triceps contracted. The wide expanse of his back powerfully flexed as he raised the tool again and again.

Although he wasn't nude, there was something voyeuristic in what I was doing. I couldn't deny I was taking pleasure in secretly snapping photos of Hassan's body in motion. My reaction hadn't been swift enough. My subject pivoted to hit another section of the wall and that was when he caught me. Camera to one eye, the other eye squinted, head tilted to the side and in the zone, I was on autopilot. A big grin on his handsome face, Hassan dropped the sledgehammer, lifted and curled his arms, striking a bodybuilder pose. I laughed and it felt good. The sun filtering through the glass window hitting his body just so encouraged me to keep on snapping shots. He was beautiful and a natural. I think he knew too. Because he indulged me, striking a few more poses before heading over to the door.

His smile was warm and welcoming when he opened the door.

"Had I known you were going to take my picture I would've worn my Sunday best."

"I've seen you in your Sunday best. I think I like what you're wearing now." Mr. Murphy was some kind of sexy, all sweaty and dirty.

In all the other times I'd stopped by to check on the progress of the work going on, Hassan hadn't been on site. Either he'd just left or hadn't arrived yet. Each time disappointment settled in my bones.

All of the appliances, banquet tables, chairs, and other left behind remnants from the catering hall had been removed. My mother had talked me into completely gutting the entire first floor, starting from scratch. When I tried to balk at the suggestion, voicing my concern about the financial investment, Mom reminded me if I was serious about making a life for me and Manny in Colemanville there was no room to half step. "Ella, your studio *must* be on par with those you've spent years visiting and admiring. Colemanville is nestled between major cities in North Carolina. Don't you want to give folks a reason to check out your part of the world?"

Mom didn't mean any harm. However, it didn't quell my rebellious streak from bubbling to the surface. "I don't have that kind of money to do what you're suggesting," I had shot back way too defensively. Her grand ideas for the gallery annoyed me not because they were bad. In fact, Chantel and I sat in the backyard several evenings ago talking and drinking wine. Everything our mother had recommended was on my wish list I shared with Chantel. My mother had done *very* well for herself in real estate. The renovations she spoke of she could easily whip out her checkbook, write a check, and not think twice about it. I didn't have that luxury.

To my mother's credit, she set down the cup of tea we were having at the kitchen table in the home I was renting from her. She glared at me for several moments. I braced myself for her direct words.

"Did I ask you what you had or didn't have?"

The sharpness of her tone made me feel like I was a child again. I got over my bruised ego when my mother laid out her plan. Mom offered to lend me the money with the condition that if the gallery and studio wasn't a success within the first five years, I'd have to pay her back whatever the current interest rate was for a business loan. Mom hadn't gotten where she was today without being shrewd in her dealings. In a way it felt like she was challenging me to put up or shut up. The following week after our conversation, she summoned me to her office for a meeting with her and her attorney to sign a contract. Failure wasn't an option. I had to make this work.

Hassan reached for my hand to guide me through the

chunks of debris on the floor. The other workers from the contracting crew Hassan recommended, Justin and Phillip, greeted me with their usual, "Hello, Ms. Ella."

After I greeted the workers, I gazed up at Hassan. He had yet to release my hand. Never one for public displays of affection, I slightly tugged my hand away. Hassan grinned at me, refusing to let me go. Heat rose up my neck and fanned out across my cheeks. *Girl, this man got you blushing.*

"What is it you had to show me?"

Hassan nodded toward the ceiling. My gaze followed his nod. My eyes opened wide in sheer delight. "Oh, my gawd! Tin ceilings! They're beautiful. You cannot..." I grabbed his thick, damp bicep. "Put sheetrock over them again. They have to be original to the building. Right?"

"Yep."

Justin came over with a rolled up sheet of paper in his hand. As he unrolled it, Hassan took hold of the other end of the paper to keep it from rolling up again.

Excited, my heart pumped wildly in my chest. "Is this the original blueprint?"

"Sure is," Justin confirmed.

The men laughed when I stomped my feet and shook my head, sending wild curls whipping all around my face. I needed to get my hands on a copy to frame and hang on the wall to preserve this piece of Colemanville's history.

Justin pointed to the bottom left corner. "Here's the date the blueprint was drawn."

"Eighteen eighty-five," I whispered in awe. "This is amazing. Justin, do you think you can get a copy of this for me?"

He rolled up the blueprint. "That won't be a problem. Hassan, me and Phillip are heading out for lunch. You want me to bring you something back?"

"Nah, I'm good. See you guys in a bit."

Justin and Phillip said their goodbyes, leaving me and

Hassan alone in silence. It wasn't necessarily an awkward silence. At least not on my end. It calmed me the same as when we were in his Mustang driving along the road adjacent to the Sims' estate.

"What do you think about the brick walls?

Hassan stepped beside me, our arms centimeters from touching. The scent of natural musk and faded sandalwood was making me lightheaded. Images of Hassan tenderly doing things that would bring my body pleasure that hadn't been done since before my pregnancy were playing out in vivid watercolors in my mind. The beads of sweat forming between my breasts had nothing to do with the July heat, but everything with the man beside me.

"Ella? Did you hear me?"

"Huh?" I couldn't look at Hassan. Granddad X would always tell me my eyes gave me away. I'd be too embarrassed if he caught on that *he* was the center of my distraction. Obviously, he was having an entire conversation with me that I had zoned out on.

Hassan chuckled and I wanted to tell him to stop it because the sound was akin to a sensual siren my body was willing to answer. And it scared me.

"What do you think about leaving the side walls brick and just putting up the sheet rock on the back wall?"

Needing to put some distance between me and Hassan, I walked around the expansive space. My gaze was drawn to the flooring. Unfortunately, it wasn't in as pristine shape as the tin ceiling and brick walls.

When I did take a chance to look at Hassan, I knew he had to see my chest fill with air and fall, freely releasing a dreamy sigh. Why was he standing there with his hands behind his back, head tilted to the side, gazing at me like I was the rarest of...heck if I knew...something extraordinary?

Tapping my finger against my pursed lips, I slowly turned

in a three-sixty. "I think I like that, Hassan. Especially with the tin ceilings. Yeah...this is going to make a beautiful art gallery. How's the upstairs looking?"

"Go on up and see for yourself."

With all the walls taken down, the staircase in the back along the right wall was fully exposed. "Oh my goodness. These steps are sturdy."

"This structure was well built. It'll be standing another hundred years."

Hassan's comment instantly made me think of my mother. Because in that moment I could see into the future with my bloodline ensuring that Ilona's legacy, my legacy, lived on. Now I understood Mom's disappointment in her daughters not wanting to join her in the real estate business. Later, I could brainstorm with Chantel to see if we could come up with a way to help our mother. Coming up on sixty, it was only a matter of time before she retired. It would be a shame to see her hard work not be carried on by someone in the family.

Like downstairs, the plaster walls were gone, exposing the brick walls. I loved the natural light filtering through the windows from the front of the room. Hassan's gaze followed me as I took my time moving around the space. The area was perfect for my art and photography studio, to give art lessons to children. During one of our afternoon Sunday lunches at my grandparents, Granddad X gave me an eight by ten framed photo of me and my great-grandmother Ilona. I couldn't have been no older than three years old. I was sitting on her lap in front of an easel. Paintbrush in hand, Ilona was guiding my chubby hand to make a brushstroke against the canvas.

"Thought you might like to have this. Mama loved teaching children to paint."

That night I took the precious photo home and set it on

my nightstand. Lying on my side, I stared at it, wishing I could remember her tender instructions.

Although offering children art lessons for a nominal fee was part of my business plan, seeing that picture of me and my great-grandmother was as if God was speaking to me. From all the stories I'd heard about Ilona, the recurring theme was that she believed everyone should be introduced to the beauty of art in one form or another, even the little ones.

"I'm pleased with how everything is turning out. Do you know when the project will be completed?" I inquired as I headed down the stairs with Hassan following me closely.

"If all goes well by late August...early September."

That would be in four to six weeks. Like I hoped, I could schedule the grand opening in the fall. Chantel had already designed invitations. And I'd been working on the guestlist, which of course included all the residents of Colemanville, folks I'd met in my travels, and friends I made while working for the NBA.

"That timeline is with adding men's and women's bathrooms downstairs and upstairs, a kitchenette on the first floor, and a sink area upstairs too?"

Hassan removed the bandana from his back pocket and wiped his forehead.

"Yes, ma'am. Justin said he doesn't have to reroute any of the plumbing or the gas line. If things go as scheduled, the materials for the bathrooms and kitchenette are due to be delivered next week. Shouldn't take long to install everything. The floors are due to be delivered in a week and half. Tomorrow Justin and Philip plan on framing out the kitchen area and bathrooms."

"Pinch me. This can't be real."

Hassan chuckled. "How about I take you to lunch instead of pinching you?"

I smiled coyly at Hassan. He and his team had thoroughly

cleaned out the trash and debris left behind. He certainly didn't have to stay behind and help Justin and Philip do demolition. I wasn't stupid as to why Hassan was tearing down walls. The man liked me. And I was smitten too.

"How about if I treat you to lunch?" I countered, making a mental note to bring Justin and Philip breakfast tomorrow.

"Lead the way."

Twelve

It was a shame there wasn't anywhere nice in Colemanville anymore to go for a meal. The diner we hung out at as teens was an empty dilapidated shell. Mom mentioned years ago trying to give it a go at hiring a staff and reopening what was once a major hub. But figured since she didn't know a thing about the restaurant business to leave it be after considering the financial investment she'd have to make.

When I didn't feel like cooking or showing up on Grandma Rose's front step to freeload, me, Manny, and Chantel traveled to either Jacksonville or Fayetteville to eat. The place I'd brought Hassan to for lunch was a quaint bistro in downtown Jacksonville. We'd placed our orders and were waiting for the server to return with our lemonades.

"How's Manny doing?"

Smiling, I told Hassan the truth. "Asking about you every five minutes."

Well maybe not every five minutes, but certainly several times a week Manny wanted to know when he would see Mr.

Hassan again. Every Sunday, Manny searched for his new friend after church. He wasn't the only one.

Hassan's smile outshined the afternoon sun, warming my insides.

"He seems like a great kid."

"He really is. And I'm not just saying that because he's mine. Manny is sweet and considerate of others. A couple years ago, I had a terrible sinus infection and could hardly get out of bed. That little boy, at five years old, looked after me."

"How so?" Hassan asked as the server placed our drinks on the table and told us our food would be out shortly.

Before explaining, I took a sip of the cool drink. Hassan's intense gaze made me thirsty.

"Where we lived at the time we had a snowstorm. Chantel was supposed to come visit, but couldn't get a flight." I recalled how helpless I had felt not being able to care for my son.

"At least she would've been able to look after Manny. A ten-minute task of making breakfast for my son turned into an hour; I was that weak and in pain. Have you ever had a sinus infection?"

Hassan shook his head. "Never."

"You don't ever want one. Feels like someone's beating you between the eyes and on top of your head."

I laughed when Hassan frowned and shook in his seat.

"Ouch."

"Yeah, ouch is right. I couldn't think straight. Barely got through scrambling eggs and making toast before I passed out on the sofa."

The tears that formed in my eyes couldn't be helped. "I woke up to Manny nudging me on the shoulder. He'd fixed us both peanut butter and jelly sandwiches with waaay too much jelly."

Reaching across the table, Hassan took my hand. "The little prince taking care of the queen."

I didn't respond. Instead, I gave him a half-hearted smile. Until now, telling this story, I hadn't realized how lacking my life was. There was no one I could call on to take care of my child when I couldn't and my sister was miles away.

The waiter coming toward us with our food was a welcomed interruption. An opportunity to steer the conversation in a different direction.

"Are you looking forward to your daughters coming in August?"

Hassan picked up the hearty brisket sandwich on brioche. I could tell he wanted to dig in, but held off to answer me.

"They're actually coming this Friday," he answered before taking a huge bite of his sandwich.

"Oh, nice. They get to spend two extra weeks with you. What do they like to do?"

I was cutting a piece of chicken in my Caesar salad when another text came through on my phone. This time it was from Victoria. Yep, she had taken to texting me unwanted messages too.

Call me, right now!

Annoyed, I turned my phone on silent. She must have thought I was crazy if she thought I was calling her.

"My oldest, Zuri, loves working with children. Every summer she volunteers to help out in Vacation Bible School with the nursery age children. Kali, my youngest, loves all kinds of animals."

"Even snakes," I squeaked out.

Hassan chuckled. "No. She says all reptiles are out of the question."

"Have you taken her to the Sims Estate to go horseback riding?"

"Every week that she's here. It's cool the Sims family has that summer and weekend equestrian program."

Fond memories of me, Jillian, and Kristen riding for hours on the estate resurfaced. "They've had that program since before I was born. Papa Packer, one of my best friends' grandfather, started the program in the mid-nineteen sixties to expose Black youth to ranching life."

"Really? I didn't know that."

"Of course you wouldn't. You're not Colemanville bred and born." Although I was teasing, I was sure pride for my birth place rang loud and clear.

Hassan's grunt made me laugh.

"Don't matter where I was born. Colemanville is my home. I'm never leaving."

I held up my glass of lemonade in a toast. Hassan clinked his glass against mine. "Yes, to never leaving."

Over lunch I learned that we were both educators at the undergraduate level. Hassan taught a course in Sustainable Materials Management at Fayetteville State University during the fall and spring semesters. Naturally, our conversation turned to what we loved most...our children.

After lunch Hassan dropped me off at my grandparents' house. When he came around to the passenger side to open the door, he took hold of my hand. Standing in the street beside his work truck, I imagined the old ladies on their front porches peeping over the tops of their glasses.

"Can I take you out Wednesday night?"

A sexy grin curled the corners of Hassan's mouth, causing me to swoon. "On a real date?"

I didn't hesitate answering. And I didn't care if my quickness came across as eager.

"What time should I be ready?"

"Six-thirty."

He leaned in and kissed me on the cheek. It was the

sweetest of kisses. If we didn't have an audience I would've kissed his full lips.

"I'll be ready."

"Hey, Grandma Rose. Whatcha watching?"

My grandmother looked up at me from her perch on the sofa. I sat beside her, kissing her soft, wrinkled cheek. Her weathered hand lovingly patted my thigh.

Instead of answering me, she peered at me for several seconds, like she was looking into my soul. "Lately you've seemed troubled. But today you seem mighty joyful. Something good happen to you?"

The corners of my mouth twitched involuntarily, forming a smile. "I had lunch with Hassan."

Grandma Rose picked up the remote and paused whatever classic black and white television show she was watching before I interrupted her.

"Oh, I see. How was your lunch date?" The twinkle in her dark eyes was too cute. She was a hopeless romantic.

"Grandma Rose, it wasn't a date. I treated him to lunch for staying around to help the contractor with demolition of the building."

She gawked at me like I had just cussed her out.

"You treated him to lunch," my grandmother scoffed, almost disgusted. "In my day womenfolk didn't buy a man's meal. The men did the buying." Grandma Rose slowly shook her head, that twinkle diminishing. "I don't know about that, Ella. I thought he was a decent man."

Grandma Rose, that is so archaic of you. I knew better to voice that out loud.

"He *is* a decent man, Grandma Rose. To set the record straight, Miss Ma'am, he did insist on paying, but I turned him down. If it makes you feel any better, Hassan invited me to dinner Wednesday night. I'm sure he's going to pay."

I couldn't help giggling when she cut her eyes at me. I knew her silence meant she was having reservations about Hassan paying for dinner. Grandma Rose picked up the remote and unpaused her show.

"I'm watching Perry Mason."

"How many times have you seen this episode?" I'd seen it at least three times as a kid sitting right here on the sofa watching it with her and my grandfather.

"Hush up. Don't worry about how many times I've seen it."

I slapped my hands on my thighs. "Welp, that's my cue to go."

Before I could get up to go search for my grandfather, there was a knock at the door.

"I'll get it."

Stunned, my feet were cemented to the floor at the unexpected visitor. We stared at each other until finally I found my voice.

"Oh, my goodness! Jillian!"

Opening the door, I stepped out on the porch. I didn't know who reached first. It didn't matter. In a locked embrace, we rocked from side to side, tears overflowing. I hadn't realized how much I'd missed my friend. Too many years had gone by without either one of us reaching out. I couldn't lay all the blame at Jillian's feet. I had kept my distance to conceal my shame. Now in hindsight, I knew Jillian and Kristen would've been there to support me.

"It's so good to see you, Jillian."

"Good to see you too, Ella. Let's sit down and catch up."

The loud volume of the television was a telltale sign Grandma Rose didn't have her hearing aids in. I could hear the television as I climbed the porch steps. There was no concern of her overhearing our conversation.

Just like old times, we swayed back and forth on the porch swing sharing secrets. Except we were grown women and not teen girls swearing each other to secrecy about our latest crushes. Jillian confided in me how she'd ended up in Colemanville because of a broken marriage and suspicions of her husband being unfaithful. I didn't judge her when she told me she and her husband were going to counseling to salvage their marriage. If they could make it work and keep their family intact, I wished Jillian the best.

My feet did a happy dance on the aged wooden planks. Jillian and her children were permanently staying in Colemanville. She was opening a day spa a block over from where I was opening the gallery. In the interim she was taking appointments for esthetician services at her parents' spacious home.

"Girl, you got any openings for next week? I could use some pampering."

Jillian bumped my shoulder with hers. "You know I got you, girl."

If I grinned any harder, my cheeks were going to crack. I was so proud of Jillian for going after what she'd been dreaming of since we were teens. We, including Kristen, spent hours in my room, cutting out pictures of beauty products from magazines. In between eating snacks and giggling, the task was left up to me to arrange the pictures in an eye-catching collage. Left up to those two, the pictures would've been haphazardly plastered all over the posterboard.

"Do you still have that collage we made?"

Jillian's blue-gray eyes glimmered. "You know I do."

A spirit of tranquility rested over us as we gazed at each other. And I knew the silent years between us were forgiven with what she said next. "I still have all the letters you wrote me too."

Summer coming to an end was dreadful. That last week before Jillian was to return north, the three of us literally spent every waking hour together. Rotating between our families' homes for sleepovers, going to the diner for banana splits, riding horses over every acreage of the Sims estate, we were inseparable. The day of Jillian's departure, we'd cry our eyes out. From late August until early June, the letter writing campaign was on. Getting a letter from Jillian was the highlight of my week. Back then Chantel was a nuisance. I would slam my bedroom door shut in her face and lock it so I could read my letters in peace.

"I kept mine, too."

Nana Flo had summoned me out to the estate days ago. She entrusted me to clean the portrait of her mother, Iva Rae. Leisurely, swinging beside my best friend, an idea for a gift popped into my head. Hopefully, Nana Flo would allow me to hold onto the portrait longer than necessary.

Jillian was just as thrilled when I told her I was opening up a gallery and studio within walking distance of where Iva's House of Beauty was located.

I didn't have to, at least not right now, especially when we hadn't seen each other in years. But I did anyway. I came clean with my childhood friend about the circumstances surrounding Manny's paternity and Preston's shenanigans. Strangely, it felt liberating laying out the messiest of the mess of my life to Jillian. There wasn't any of the shame I'd experienced when telling my sister. Perhaps because at some level as a mother and her experienced turmoil with her husband, I believed Jillian understood why and how I had put up with Preston's egregious behavior.

"Oh, honey. I'm so sorry. I wish I had been there to support you."

Jillian hugged me tightly, absorbing weariness from my bones.

"I know you would've been there. And Kristen too."

"Girl, you know we would've done worse to Pathetic Preston than we did to Butthead Brian."

Jillian rolled her eyes. "Dumping me for Wendy."

I pressed my lips together and looked away from Jillian. It was horrible what we did. In our defense, Brian deserved it. Kristen was the mastermind behind operation revenge. That summer Jillian discovered Brian dumped her for Wendy, he was working cutting neighbors' lawns. He was one of the few kids with a cell phone at that time. On just about every pole in Colemanville, he had a flier posted with his number advertising his one-man landscaping business. Disguising our voices we made appointments to have yard work done at other people's homes. In a tightly knit community like ours, it wasn't unusual for a service to be provided prior to payment. Brian would head to homes in the community, doing his best tidying up lawns and trimming shrubbery with the promise of his payment being in the mailbox. That was my idea.

When I couldn't hold it any longer, I burst out laughing and so did Jillian. "Why'd we let Kristen talk us into doing that prank?"

"I don't know. But I did feel a little bit guilty when he opened all those envelopes only to find Monopoly money."

I cracked up again. "You only felt guilty because you still liked him."

"Girl, you know my heart was broken over that slick behind Brian."

Jillian leaned forward to peep at the screen door. She lowered her voice when she spoke. "Girl, Wendy is my cousin."

"Are you serious? How?"

Intrigued, I listened as Jillian shared with me how her great-grandfather Doctor Everett Mercer was white passing and had a white family over in Jacksonville. His daughter by the white wife was Nana Flo's half-sister and Wendy's grandmother. I almost fell off the swing when she told me that the marriage to the white wife wasn't legal because the good old doctor was actually married to Iva Rae first. My heart went out to Wendy that her grandmother would disown her if she forged a relationship with the Black side of her family.

"Whew, girl…that's sure 'nough is something else. Kristen and I always said you and Wendy favored. Is she still a mean girl?"

Laughing, Jillian said, "No, she's not. We've been getting to know each other. It's been real nice."

"I'm glad Wendy has you, Jillian."

"Yeah, me too. Listen, I have to go. I have to get back to Mom's for my two-thirty appointment."

We both stood and hugged one more time. We went our separate ways with the promise of getting together for dinner.

Thirteen

I didn't know who was calling me nonstop. That was a lie. It had to be one of two people. Irritated, I balanced the box my grandfather had given me that belonged to Ilona on my knee to open the front door. Chantel was pacing and looked like she wanted to kill somebody.

"What's wrong?"

"I've been trying to call you! Preston was here!"

Bewildered, I stared at my sister. "Here?"

"Yes! He tried to snatch Manny!"

Fingers weak, the box slipped from my hands and went crashing to the floor.

"Oh, my God! Where's Manny?! Where's my baby?!"

Chantel grabbed me by the hands and led me over to the sofa. I didn't want to sit down. I pulled away. The shrill sound coming out of me was foreign to my own ears. Tears blurred my vision. "Where's Manny?! Where's my baby?!"

"He's upstairs in his room with Mom and Dad."

My shoulders sagged in relief. "What happened? Where is Preston?"

"Mrs. Winters across the street noticed a dark gray car that kept circling our street while I was in the backyard playing with Manny and Noah. Manny and Noah heard the ice cream truck and went around to the front of the house. I swear Ella, I was only in the house for no more than two minutes to get money. When I came out to buy the boys ice cream, Preston had his hand over Manny's mouth and was trying to put him in his car. I jumped on his back and started kicking Preston's ass."

She held her fist up to show me the bruises on her knuckles. I noticed her elbow was scraped up pretty badly too.

In the seriousness of the moment, Chantel laughed. "Manny and Noah called themselves helping me fight. One of them got tangled up between me and Preston. I tripped and fell on the ground. Preston fell on top of me. That nigga tried to choke me."

"What?!" I officially hated Preston.

"Girl, I said *tried*. Manny clamped down on his thigh like a pit bull. Noah bit him good on the shoulder. Preston started screaming and cussing like a little bitch."

My voice hitched even higher. "Did he hit those babies?"

"No, the police ran up on us. Yanked me off of the ground and handcuffed him."

Chantel reached in her back pocket. "Here's the cop's card. Jackass is being arrested for attempted kidnapping."

I took the card, torn between going down to the police precinct to see Preston behind bars for myself or going upstairs to see about Manny. My maternal instincts won. Standing rooted in place, I took several deep breaths to get myself together before going to see my son. Chantel was behind me, rubbing soothing circles on my back.

"Ella, he's safe. Manny is safe."

"I know." I turned to my sister and hugged her. "Thanks for protecting him."

Her voice cracked. "Always. I would never let anything happen to Manny."

If I knew nothing else, I knew Chantel would lay her life down for Manny.

"I know you wouldn't."

Releasing Chantel, I made my way upstairs with her on my heels. Manny was sitting between my parents on the bed. When he saw me, he jumped up and ran to me. Dropping to my knees, I grabbed him and wept like I'd never done before. The sheer terror that ran through me when I thought Preston had taken Manny. In those few seconds all sorts of horrible things ran through my mind. Not for one minute did I believe it wasn't beneath Preston to harm Manny.

"Mommy, that man tried to take me."

Gently holding Manny away from me, I stared into his eyes. "You don't remember your father?"

Manny shook his head.

From the doorway, Chantel mumbled, "Thank God."

"That's a blessing," my mom tagged on.

I was still too shaken up to tell Chantel and Mom to sensor their words in front of Manny. All too soon, he would know the truth. I wanted his innocence to stay intact for as long as possible.

Stubbornly, Manny shook his head again. "I don't want him for my father. He's mean..." Manny's bottom lip quivered. "And scary."

Mom and Chantel rushed over to where Manny and I were and kneeled down in front of him. Mom tenderly rubbed her hand over Manny's cheek that still held some chubbiness to it. "It's okay to be scared, Manny. I'm scared sometimes too." Mom looked at Dad. "But I have people who love me so being scared isn't too much for me. You have all of us who love you so it's not too much for you, either."

"And you know you can sleep with me every night."

Chantel tickled his stomach, causing Manny to laugh. "We can watch cartoons and eat popcorn all night."

Manny's eyes went wide. "Can I, Mommy?"

I pursed my lips. "I don't know about every night."

Silent the entire time, Dad stood abruptly. "I'm going down to that precinct."

Dad's nostrils were flared. His hands balled into fists at his side. Chantel and I helped my mother stand. Going over to Dad, she grabbed his hands.

"Owen, don't do anything you'll get yourself in trouble for."

"Rosaline, I wouldn't be a man if I didn't step to that son of a bitch for what he did to my baby. And for trying to kidnap my grandson."

Dad kissed Mom on the cheek then Manny on the forehead. When he got across the threshold, Mom gave me a panicked look. "Ella, go with your father. He'll listen to you."

The entire ride over to the precinct Dad was silent. His hands gripped the steering wheel as he drove. Always the calm, level headed parent, Dad's approach to conflict was to talk through it. Silence meant he was calculating his next move. Turning off the ignition, Dad glared at me and it broke my heart.

"Ella, you should've told me what that bastard did to you. I would've handled him."

By handle I knew my dad meant to beat Preston within an inch of his life. It wouldn't have been the first time he put hands on someone because of one of his daughters.

In high school, Chantel was sweet on some guy from the rival school in Jacksonville. He came from money and had the reputation of being a bad boy. My sister had always had a smart mouth on her. She had said something the guy didn't like. His response was to backhand Chantel across the face. Chantel didn't come home crying. Like earlier, she had put up a good fight.

Where Chantel and I differed was that my sister could care less about being embarrassed. When she came home, face bruised, she had no qualms with telling our mother how she had gotten the black and blue marks and who put them there. Mom had called Dad. He took one look at his youngest daughter and demanded Chantel take him to the guy's home. My dad's intent was to talk to his parents. When Dad, Mom, and Chantel arrived at the guy's house, he was leaning against his car talking crap with his friends. He told my dad to go to hell when Dad demanded he go get his parents.

Simpleton made the mistake, because he was at six-four, of bucking at my dad and called him "a stupid ass old man." His biggest error was thinking he could swing on my dad just because his parents were in the doorway watching, condoning their son's disrespect. He thought differently when he found himself laid out flat on the sidewalk, staring up at the stars.

If Dad had done that to a loud-mouthed teen who hit his youngest daughter, he surely would've done a lot worse to Preston. Although my dad had been defending himself against that teen, that didn't stop his parents from pressing charges against my father and my dad spending the night in jail and having to get a lawyer. In the end the charges were dropped when the truth came out after my parents pressed charges against the teen for hitting Chantel.

I wouldn't be able to live with myself if my father ended up in serious trouble because of me.

"Daddy, that's why I didn't come to you. I knew what you would've done."

Hand on the door handle, Dad stared at me. "I would've killed him."

Police Chief Zachary Leonard was at the desk in the one

floor building when we entered. Every teen girl in town had a crush on the police chief. The lawman was tall, brawny, and beyond handsome. Didn't matter that he had gone to school with our parents and had a wife and six kids at home.

Chief Zachary rested his elbow on the desk and looked from me to my dad. "Ella...Owen. What can I do for you?"

"Zach, I think you know why we're here."

Standing, Chief Leonard rapped his knuckles on the desk. "I do. Owen, we go way back and I understand—"

"Then you'll understand I need a word with that bastard."

Chuckling, the chief scratched at the back of his neck. "Listen...I feel you, man. But you know I can't let you do that."

"Chief Leonard, he tried to kidnap my son. Will you at least let me speak to him?" I knew I was grabbing at straws in the dark.

My phone rang. Out of habit I glanced at it and saw it was Victoria again. Instead of ignoring it, I answered because there had to be a reason why she was persistent with trying to reach me.

Fourteen

"Mommy! Mr. Hassan is here!" Manny ran into the kitchen, where I was at the stove cooking breakfast, obviously excited over the impromptu visit.

"Oh, no," I groaned, wiping the back of my hand over my forehead. I looked terrible, not in any condition to receive a guest. My hair was unruly. Drawing a shaky breath, I glanced down at the way too big t-shirt and basketball shorts covering me. I was sure dark circles were under my eyes.

Sleep didn't come easy last night. It wasn't because I was worried about Preston. Chief Leonard told me and Dad once Preston's bail was posted he couldn't force him out of town. But promised that he and the other officers would make Preston's time in Colemanville unwelcoming. "Don't worry, Ella and Owen. Me and my men gotcha covered." The chief had locked eyes with my father. "Owen, if he comes around and we're not there...do what you have to do to protect your family."

What had me twisting and turning in my bed and getting up every hour to check on Manny was why Victoria had been blowing up my phone. She was desperately trying to reach me to warn me of Preston's plan to take Manny out of the country. My legs had felt like they were kicked from underneath me. I had challenged Victoria because I didn't believe her. For all I knew she was in on the kidnapping plot. "How is that even possible? Preston doesn't have Manny's passport."

I felt sick to my stomach with what Victoria had said next. "Preston was aware of your every move, Ella. He let you believe he didn't know where you were... What you were doing." She had named the last three states Manny and I lived in to prove to me she was telling the truth.

While packing for our move from Nashville to Colemanville I couldn't find our passports, which I thought was weird. I'd kept them in a legal envelope in my lingerie drawer. I had torn our apartment up looking for the important documents, wracking my brain trying to remember if I had put them somewhere else.

I almost vomited at the thought of my personal space being invaded by some unknown figure going through my things, touching my personal belongings.

"Why? Why does he want Manny now?" I had hysterically demanded.

Victoria swore she didn't know what was going on. "All I know is that he's been talking crazy about people wanting to bring him down. You being one of those people. To keep you quiet he was going to take Manny. I wanted to warn you."

If I could've gotten my hands on Victoria and Preston, I would've choked them both. "Why? Why should I believe anything you're saying? *You* and Preston tried to ruin me in the art community."

There was a deafening silence before the woman who I had thought was a friend spoke.

"Preston isn't the man I thought he was... No child should be taken from his mother."

That was all Victoria had said before abruptly hanging up and leaving me with more questions than answers.

"Mommy? Did you hear me?"

"Yes, baby, I heard you." I tucked my conversation with Victoria away to dissect and examine later.

"You took so long coming into the living room, I brought Hassan back," Chantel explained before calling Manny out of the kitchen.

Hassan's intense gaze roamed over me. Concern was etched across his handsome features.

"Are you okay? I heard what happened with Manny," he commented once Chantel and Manny were gone.

I inhaled deeply and let out a long breath. Small town living. Everybody knew your business before dawn. My voice quivered with the lie. "I'm good." I wasn't good. That man had my child's and *my* passport in his possession. He had planned to take my son out of the country. And there would've been nothing I could've done about it at that moment.

After I had hung up with Victoria, my first order of business was to go online and report that our passports were missing to the U.S. Department of State, something I should've done months ago.

"Are you sure, Ella?"

A single tear ran down my cheek. I couldn't control my quivering bottom lip. "He tried to take my baby."

Before I could take another breath, Hassan was holding me in his arms. My entire body went limp beneath the weight of my current situation. What was I supposed to do? Instinct told me to take my son and run like I always had done. My running wouldn't stop Preston from chasing after me and Manny like a jackal hunting an antelope. The thought of it made me bury my face in Hassan's chest and sob.

"Shh, I got you," Hassan murmured. His tenderly spoken

words made me cry even harder. I'd never had a man tell me that. I couldn't explain why I believed him. Perhaps it was in the way he held me close. My bridge over troubled water, slowly swaying me from side to side so I wouldn't break.

As screwed up as my life was right about now, that peace I felt with Hassan on that Sunday afternoon as we drove through the countryside seeped into my bones. If there were such a thing as making a wish come true, I would wish to reside in that space and time with my baby where Preston didn't exist.

Hassan released me. His large hands framed my face. The way he gazed into my eyes took my breath away.

"I mean it, Ella. If you or Manny need anything, all you have to do is ask. Okay?"

"Okay...thank you."

Hassan's tender kiss to my forehead was more than enough to seal his promise.

"Do you want to stay for breakfast?"

The least I could do was feed him after drenching his shirt in my tears. I had no control of the butterflies fluttering in my stomach making me feel like I was seventeen again when Hassan grinned at me.

"Depends on what you're fixing."

Despite knowing I looked a scruffy mess, I grinned back at him.

"Scrambled eggs with cheese, turkey sausage, and Belgian waffles. All Manny's favorites."

"Then I'm staying."

Of course Manny was thrilled with Hassan joining us for breakfast. He jibber-jabbered nonstop as we ate our meal, for which I was grateful because he seemed to be back to himself.

"Mr. Hassan, do you have any children I can play with?"

Cutting into his waffle, Hassan smiled at Manny. "I have two daughters, Zuri and Kali. They're thirteen and eleven."

We all laughed when Manny mumbled an uninterested, "Oh."

"Manny, what's wrong with girls?" Chantel challenged, her eyebrows raised, making a goofy face.

Exasperated, Manny threw his hands up. "Everything. Girls don't like doing nothing."

"Like what don't girls like doing?" Hassan asked as he was putting a piece of waffle drenched in syrup in his mouth.

Manny furrowed his forehead as if thinking before making his case. "Climbing trees, going fishing, riding a bike. They don't like nothing."

"Not true. My youngest daughter Kali loves doing all those things."

Eyes wide in unexpected excitement, Manny dropped his fork on the table. "For real, Mr. Hassan? Do you think she would want to go with me, and Granddad, and Granddad X fishing?"

"I'll ask her and see what she says." Hassan looked over the table at me and held my gaze. "Or maybe you can ask her yourself when she comes to visit in a few days."

"Yes! I always have fun with..."

I didn't have the heart to tell Manny to take it down a notch. He'd been through a traumatizing event. But I'd rather have him talk nonstop than be withdrawn and frightened. A knock at the door caused everyone to stop talking.

Chantel pushed away from the table before standing. "I'll go see who it is."

Moments later my grandparents and Manny's buddy Noah came trailing behind Chantel. Granddad X held a shotgun and Grandma Rose a metal baseball bat. I must've made some kind of face because Chantel and Hassan were cracking up.

"Manny, take Noah up to your room to play."

"Yes, Mommy."

Before exiting, Manny grabbed two sausage links. He handed one to Noah before hugging and kissing his great-grandparents.

When I was certain the boys were out of seeing and hearing distance, I turned to my grandparents.

"Granddad X, why did you bring that shotgun? Grandma Rose, what are you going to do with that bat?"

It wasn't unusual that my grandfather owned a rifle. Most of the older generations kept one for hunting and protection. Not protection from the community, but those *other* folks who attempted a time or two to step foot in Colemanville kicking up trouble. What was unusual was that he brought one into my home. I never had firearms around my son. And particularly didn't care for Granddad X toting his rifle in my home.

"I bought it in case that good for nothing piece of a man shows up around here," Granddad X fussed as he pulled out a chair for Grandma Rose to sit at the kitchen table.

"Your mama and daddy told us what happened." Grandma Rose took my hand, tears in her eyes.

Panic skated up my spine. I shot Chantel a look. How much had Mom and Dad told my grandparents? It felt like my breakfast was about to come back up.

Hassan must've sensed my uneasiness. I was tongue-tied and didn't know how to respond to my grandmother.

He looked at me and made his announcement. "I'm gonna head out. Have to stock the fridge before the girls arrive on Friday."

Needing a second to get myself together, I got up to see Hassan to the door.

"Mr. X and Ms. Rose, take care." His smile was charming when he eyed Grandma Rose. "Be careful with that bat."

"Oh, I will be *extra* careful, young man."

Chantel rolled her eyes at our grandmother's coy tittering.

"Youngin', get on out of here flirting with my woman." The crinkles at the corners of Granddad X's eyes were made from his grinning.

Hassan held his hands up in surrender. "Don't want no trouble. I'm going, sir."

When we reached the front door, Hassan took my hand. "I meant what I said, Ella. Call me if you need anything."

"Thank you, Hassan."

Too old to play games, I spoke what was on my heart. "I appreciate you coming over to check on me and Manny. It means a lot."

I willingly went when Hassan pulled me in even closer and placed a tender kiss on my lips. There were times when I tried to date but couldn't mentally get past the simplest intimate gestures like holding hands. I would clam up and make excuses to back away. With Hassan, it was different. I was different. Being without male companionship wasn't something I missed having in my life until now. I craved companionship.

"Are you still up for going out tomorrow? I'd understand if you want to stay home."

Although my desire was to spend time with Hassan, my first instinct was to say I would stay home, purely operating out of fear that Preston would attempt to do something stupid again once he was released. But that wasn't any kind of way to live. I refused to live my life looking over my shoulder.

Mom had insisted on Manny and I staying with her until we knew Preston was out of Colemanville. I refused to leave my home. Unrelenting, Mom wore me down until I agreed to Manny rotating between staying home with me and with her and Dad. Manny would be with my parents on Wednesday and Thursday. There was no need for me to not keep my date with Hassan.

"Yes, I'd love to keep our date. Manny will be with my parents."

"I'll pick you up at six."

"I'll be ready." I couldn't resist kissing Hassan again. This time our lips lingered a little longer.

Grandma Rose was sipping on a glass of pineapple juice when I returned. Granddad X was looking straight through my soul. Before my behind could hit the seat, the old man started in on me with his inquisition.

"What else is going on, Ella? I know it's more than that man trying to take Manny. Rosaline was tightlipped about it. Said it wasn't her story to tell."

I appreciated my mother honoring my confidentiality. Yet, this is one time I wished she hadn't. *Help me, Lord*.

Grandma Rose's words broke me. "Baby, there's nothing you can't tell me and your granddaddy." She looked at Chantel. "That goes for you too."

Chantel read my mind. I was torn. What if what I had to say was too much for them? Sure, my grandparents were healthy octogenarians, could still do things that folks twenty years younger were doing. That didn't stop me from wanting to protect them from ugliness I knew was bound to trouble them.

"Ella, Granddad X and Grandma Rose are strong. They can handle the truth. It's time our entire inner circle knows everything."

Fifteen

Weeks had gone by since I told my grandparents *everything*. As Chantel predicted, they handled the news without crumbling. However, that didn't stop them from giving me a tongue lashing and accusing me of being prideful and not depending on them during my time of crisis.

"We're your family, Ella. My gut told me there was something to you moving around like you had gypsy in your blood," Granddad X had grumbled.

"You know pride is a sin," my sweet, gentle grandmother followed up, causing me to feel ten times worse.

My grandparents had zeroed in, further exposing me, making me face my flaws. I had believed I deserved to wallow in my distress. Never considered that my actions were prideful or hurtful to those who loved me. Deep down inside I was resentful of Granddad X and Grandma Rose calling me out. But after a long discussion over lunch with Chantel and Jillian, they helped me see things from my grandparents' perspective. I had caused myself years of undue stress when I had support. Unfortunately, I was too concerned that my perfect image would be shattered.

True to Chief Leonard's word, when Preston was released from jail, his every move was monitored. Preston wasn't given a slap on the wrist. He was charged with attempted kidnapping. At his arraignment the district attorney decided to enhance the charges with the evidence presented that Preston's plan was to take Manny out of the country. In the trunk of Preston's rental car, he had a suitcase with clothes for him and Manny, their passports, and plane tickets to Mali. He had planned to take my baby to Africa! I almost fainted when Silas whispered in my ear at the arraignment that Preston most likely chose Mali because there was no extradition treaty with the United States. If his plan hadn't been foiled, it could've been years before I would've seen Manny again.

The magistrates' warning left no room for misinterpretation.

"Here in Colemanville, we take care of our own. You made a mistake coming into our town, attempting to kidnap a child and take him from his mother. A daughter of Colemanville."

Of course Preston, with his smug self, pleaded not guilty. And had the nerve to wink at me when he left the courthouse. It took two court officers and Silas to hold my dad back from going after Preston.

Although I did have legal custody of Manny, Silas made some calls to get us in front of the judge days later to issue an emergency custody order. This would prevent Preston from taking Manny out of the state. We agreed our strategy had to be to keep my son safe. I was still confused as to what Preston's agenda was. Victoria hadn't called me again. I was tempted to contact her to press her for information. Silas had advised against. "We don't know if she had a role in any of this."

My gut was telling me she knew more than she was letting

on. Chantel had hypothesized that whatever it was, that it was serious and Victoria was scared to reveal it.

With all the turmoil in my life I did make space for my budding relationship with Hassan. Our first date was memorable and reminiscent of something out of a Hallmark romance movie. Hassan was punctual with a bouquet of flowers. He had taken great care with his attire. I liked that his locs were loose and his beard trimmed. The crisp, white, short-sleeved dress shirt magnified his dark, sun kissed skin. He hugged me tightly. The intoxicating scent of his cologne prolonged my hold on him. I didn't want to let him go because in his arms I felt weightless.

Hassan took me to a French restaurant in downtown Fayetteville. After dinner, we strolled, holding hands and looking in the windows of the shops. One of them we stopped in and picked up graphic t-shirts for his daughters and Manny. We stumbled upon a long line of folks on the sidewalk waiting to get ice cream from a parlor that had been there dating back to the nineteen fifties. That night I learned Hassan's favorite flavor was butter pecan.

Considerate as ever, Hassan hadn't kept me from home too long. I wanted to protest when he commented, "Let me get you home at a decent hour."

Manny was with my parents and I didn't have a curfew. Maybe it was me constantly looking at my phone that prompted Hassan to end our date earlier than I would've liked. Part of me was resentful that my life was being controlled by a man I had never had an intimate relationship with in the first place. Another part of me was afraid that my drama would push Hassan away, but he hadn't budged. Nor had he asked for details of my personal life. I was grateful. I wasn't ready to let him into that part of my life just yet.

The tapping on the glass window pulled me out of my reverie. Chantel was holding up a bag with my lunch. Dropping the broom, I ran to unlock the door. I hadn't taken the time to eat breakfast before heading out for an hour drive to do a photoshoot. Twin sisters were having babies due to be born one week apart. They'd had a horrible experience with their previous photographer and had stumbled upon my website when researching photographers in the area. I usually didn't take last minute jobs, but after hearing their story I was moved to help them. Desperate, they didn't balk at the fee I quoted for the last minute booking. The sisters were willing to pay that plus extra for me to travel to them as they were in their third trimester.

Once I was done with the photoshoot, I made my way over to the gallery. As promised, the renovations were completed with only a few minor setbacks. The appliances for the kitchen area had been on backorder for two weeks and were delivered an hour ago. I had just finished breaking down the cardboard boxes that the stove, microwave, and refrigerator had come in. My next task was to sweep the floor.

Chantel handed me the bag with my food, but held onto my drink.

"Thanks for picking up lunch for me."

"Why wouldn't I pick up lunch for you? You're my favorite sister." She took a sip from the cup. No wonder she held onto it. *Greedy*.

"I'm your only sister. Stop drinking my lemonade. Come upstairs. I want to show you something."

"It really looks nice in here, Ella. Reminds me of that gallery we went to in Nice."

Hungry, I unwrapped the sandwich as we stood in front of two easels. "Thanks, I'm pleased with how it turned out."

I took a bite of the sandwich, trying to remember which gallery she was referring to. "You mean the one with that watercolor painting by LoLo Rivers?"

"Yep, that's the one." Chantal nodded toward the covered easels. Is this what you have to show me?"

"Un-huh. Take the sheet off the one to the left first."

Carefully, Chantel removed the covering to reveal the portrait of Ms. Iva Rae I'd been painstakingly cleaning for weeks. Section by section of the painting had to be carefully brushed with a soft bristled brush to remove the collected dust.

"She was one gorgeous lady. It's crazy how much Jillian looks like her."

"I know. Except the eyes. Now uncover the other one."

I didn't have to tell Chantel to remove the covering just as gently. It was as if she knew something precious was beneath.

"O. M. G. Ella, how did you do that?"

Chantel turned to me with her mouth hanging open in temporarily stunned silence.

"I mean the portraits look almost identical. If you didn't make Ms. Iva Rae's pink blouse a deeper shade..." Tears pooled in Chantel's eyes. "Anyone would believe they were painted by the same artist. You definitely have the Ilona gene."

My cheeks grew warm from my sister's compliment. Chantel, I believed, was the only one in my family who truly knew how much I aspired to be like our great-grandmother.

"Stop it. You got the gene too!"

Chantel shook her head. "No, sis, something extra was sprinkled on you. Jillian is going to freak out when you present this at the exhibit."

With Nana Flo's blessing, I recreated the portrait of Iva Rae my great-grandmother had painted of her friend. The portrait had hung in Iva's House of Beauty until Nana Flo closed the shop almost two decades ago. My plan was to put it on exhibit in the fall with the rest of my artwork. After the exhibit, I was gifting it to Jillian to hang in her day spa.

"I hope so."

Jillian and I kept our promise and had met up for lunch and dinner a few times. Wendy had joined us for one of our lunch dates. Admittedly, it was a bit awkward at first. I had to check myself and remember we were kids back then. And as grown women there was no need to hold grudges. Before lunch was over, the three of us were laughing and having a good time. I could see why Jillian had become fond of her cousin.

Despite our busy schedules, Jillian and I managed quick phone calls and texts during the week. It felt good rebuilding our friendship.

"What do you have going on later?" Chantel inquired as she delicately covered the portraits.

"Hassan and I are taking the kids to movie night on Copper Lake after we have dinner."

Every Friday evening at dusk, the community gathered at Copper Lake to watch movies on a jumbotron screen. Although the movies were sometimes decades old, the children enjoyed them.

"Look at y'all acting like a little family and everything," Chantel teased.

"Yeah, now that Zuri has warmed up to me."

Hassan's oldest daughter gave me the cold shoulder when he introduced us the week she and Kali had arrived. Kali, on the other hand, was sweet and shy.

It was clear Zuri wasn't feeling me which had taken me by surprise. Mostly because I hadn't given her a reason to dislike me. I assumed they would have taken to me the same as Manny had done with Hassan. It was okay that Zuri hadn't. However, what I wasn't going to tolerate was her flippant mouth. Hassan was running late one afternoon and asked me to pick the girls up from the summer camp our church sponsored. Instead of taking the kids back to my house, I decided to treat them to Sims' Dairy for ice cream. Little Miss Zuri called herself chastising me when I told Kali she could have sprinkles on her ice cream. "She can't eat that. My mom said she's too fat."

Although I didn't believe in physical punishment, I wanted to give that child an old

fashioned tail whipping. I didn't like that she had spoken that way to her sister in a public setting. At the sight of tears welling up in Kali's eyes, I had put my arm around her to comfort her.

Nor did I like the tone Zuri had taken with me. Made me want to slap the taste out of her mouth. The chubby kid until I hit puberty inside of me wouldn't hold her tongue. "That's not very sisterly of you to shame Kali in public. That's not how sisters treat each other. You're supposed to have each other's backs."

What had started as a spur of the moment surprise ended in Kali changing her mind about the ice cream. Bless Manny's little heart. On our way out of the dairy, he reached for Kali's hand as we walked to the car. The ride back to my place was sullen. I didn't care about being labeled a snitch. When Hassan arrived to gather the girls, I told him what happened. To his credit, and as I expected, he made Zuri apologize to me and Kali.

I hadn't seen the girls again until the following Sunday at church. Miss Zuri was pleasant enough. Kali lavished me and Manny with hugs.

"You did right by putting her little stank behind in her place. She better be glad I wasn't there. I would've popped her in her forehead."

Laughing, I chastised Chantel. "Girl, you can't go putting your hands on folks' kids."

"Shoot, we would get our hind parts whipped by Mrs. Jones down the street from Grandma Rose and Granddad X if she *thought* we were outside cutting up."

"Gurrl, sho 'nuff. And we knew better than to sass grown folk."

Chantel followed me back downstairs. "Don't you want to help me finish cleaning up in here?" I gave her a pitiful look as I took another bite of my sandwich.

"Nope. I have to go to the market to get some things for dinner."

"Please," I whined.

Backing away from me, Chantel shook her head. "Sorry, Sis. Not in the cleaning mood."

She laughed at me when I threw a balled up napkin at her that didn't go nowhere.

A KNOCK at the door interrupted us as we moved about the kitchen.

"That's probably Hassan and the girls."

Chantel went to answer the door while I stayed behind in the kitchen putting the finishing touches on the taco bar I had prepared on the long countertop. The kids enjoyed tacos and insisted on having them every Friday. I made a healthier version with ground turkey and shredded chicken breasts for the protein. Greek yogurt was substituted for sour cream and low fat shredded cheese. Chantel made homemade salsa and guacamole. The fresh strawberry lemonade was sweetened with Splenda. No one knew the difference, except my sister.

Hassan sauntered into the kitchen with his locs pulled back dressed in a T-shirt, cargo shorts, and slides. He must've gone to the barber because his hairline was shaped up. My lip curled up in a smile at the bag he held in his hand from the candle shop we had gone inside of on our first date in Fayetteville.

"Is that for me?" I asked coyly, making my way the short distance to him.

"Depends..." He held the bag away when I reached for it. "If your kiss is as sweet as the last one."

Giggling, I promised, "It is."

The kiss was sweet and brief. Both of us were mindful that the kids were in the other room. I wasted no time peeping in the bag to see which scented candle he had brought me.

"Oh, Hassan." Removing the lid I inhaled the candle. It smelled like fresh air and the ocean. I threw my arms around his neck. "Thank you."

"Can we eat now? We're hungry," Manny interrupted.

"Yep. Y'all go upstairs and wash your hands first."

"I'm going too," Hassan said, following Manny and Kali. Zuri stayed behind.

"Ms. Ella, can I talk to you about something later...maybe tomorrow?"

I leaned against the counter to stare at her. Zuri's fingers twisted the hem of her blouse.

"Sounds serious. You want to talk now?"

Zuri's gaze shot to the direction of the stairs. "I don't want my dad around."

An uneasiness crept over me. I wanted to press her for more, but Manny was charging down the steps. The others would soon be behind him. Chantel was coming into the kitchen with Silas on her heels to join us for tacos.

All throughout dinner, I tried not to let my mind run wild with ugly thoughts of what Zuri wanted to talk to me about. I prayed I wouldn't have to tell Hassan something that would shatter his world.

Sixteen

The cool breeze from the lake made the mid-August heat tolerable. We found a spot under a tree to watch the movie. Branches gently swaying provided additional comfort. At sunset, lightning bugs came out to play, punctuating glowing flashes of light in the night air. On lightweight quilts not far from me and Hassan lounged our children, plus Noah. Hassan's head laid in my lap as we watched The Lion King. Well, I was watching because it was one of my favorites. My...I didn't know what Hassan was because we hadn't labeled whatever we were doing. All I knew was that I felt safe with Hassan. And for now that was enough.

"You okay?" Hassan inquired with his eyes closed. His breathing was slow and even.

"I thought you were sleeping."

"Off and on." He grabbed my hand and kissed it before resting it on his chest. "I was trying to sleep, but I can tell you're tense about something."

He was right. I tried pushing what Zuri wanted to confide in me to the back of my mind but I couldn't. The fact that she didn't want her father to know what was obviously troubling her was unsettling. Now, I had to quickly figure out if I should say something to him or not. Maybe my mind was working overtime and it wasn't as ominous as I was thinking.

"Just thinking about a conversation I need to have with someone." For now, I went with being vague and protecting Zuri. After our little hiccup and her apology, I didn't hold it against her. And she hadn't been disrespectful after that incident.

Hassan's eyes opened and he tilted his head to gaze at me. "Try not to stress about it. I'm sure you'll work it out...whatever it is."

Leaning down, I kissed his forehead. "I hope so."

For the remainder of the movie, I relaxed and told myself I needed to be present with the people I cared about. As I watched the girls with Manny and Noah, it wasn't the first time I noticed how they acted like mama bears over the boys. Like now, Kali was wiping down their hands with wet ones. Zuri worked at opening individual popcorn bags and inserting straws in juice boxes. Once their hands were cleaned, Zuri handed the treats to the boys. Both boys were capable of executing the simple tasks for themselves. I supposed the seven-year-olds were still in the adorably cute and tolerable phase to the girls.

"Your girls are good with Manny and Noah. They're so patient with them."

Hassan chuckled. "Kali wants to know if we could keep Manny."

I laughed too. "What did you tell her? I hope that my child wasn't a puppy."

What Hassan said next took my breath away.

"I told her only if I could keep his mother...that is if she wants to keep me too."

His dark eyes stared at me as if I was the most beautiful woman on the planet. Moments ago, I'd pondered what it was we were doing. I couldn't say that I loved Hassan...yet. Other than being physically attractive to him, I found Hassan to be kind, thoughtful, and dependable. The way he loved his girls and treated my son was enough to make me fall in love with him one day.

I wanted to lean down and *really* kiss *my* man. Too many young and old eyes were peeping at us. The last thing I wanted or needed was to be labeled indecent. Instead, the kiss was quick and chaste.

"I'll keep you for as long as you'll let me."

"Same here."

Content silence drifted over us, encasing us in our own private bubble.

"Do you think Chantel would watch the kids for a few days next week? I'd love to have some alone time with you."

Hassan was all up in my brain. With our work schedules and entertaining the children, we hardly had any alone time. Other than a few moments here and there, stealing sweet kisses when the kids weren't looking, our time was spent doing activities with the kids, which was amazing. It allowed me and his girls to bond and Manny to bond with Hassan. Wednesday evenings, Hassan and I had agreed to wrap up whatever we were doing to have game night with the kids. We alternated between his home and mine, playing board games from back in the day. I had to admit that I did like the electronic version of Monopoly. The kids got a kick out of playing Operation.

To be kid-free for a few days with Hassan would be a dream. But I didn't want to interfere with his limited time with his children. In two weeks, they'd be headed back home with their mother. He wouldn't see them again until Thanksgiving.

"She would. But do you want to wait until the girls go back home with their mother?"

"No, I don't." Hassan sat up and leaned his forehead

against mine. "Spending a few days alone with you is something I want to do for us."

I wasn't about to argue with Hassan. It wasn't like I had never been separated from Manny for short periods of time. There'd been assignments I'd taken in the past as a freelance photographer that were better for me to be alone so I could focus and not worry about when I was going to get back to the hotel with my son. Obviously, Zuri and Kali were used to being separated from Hassan for periods of time.

"Okay, I'll ask Chantel."

"WELL, IT'S ABOUT DAMN TIME!" Chantel slapped her hand on the countertop, causing me and my mother to laugh.

Mom picked up her mug and put it to her lips before taking a sip of coffee. "I agree with your sister. Go and have fun with Hassan." Mom reached across the table to squeeze my hand. "Baby, you deserve it."

Last night, as I laid in bed staring at the ceiling, I contemplated if I should tell Hassan about my history with Preston or wait until later. What if this thing between us doesn't work out? Then I would've shared my trauma with a man I no longer had a connection to. What would it be like running into him at church? The supermarket? The gas station?

"Do y'all think I should tell Hassan about Preston?" I hadn't realized I was gripping my mug until my mother laid her hand on top of mine.

"Baby, what's your heart telling you?"

Emotional, tears welled up in my eyes. "That I want to be honest with him."

"Then tell him," Chantel advised.

"What if he can't handle my past?"

"Then he's not deserving of my child. And I'll never give him business again."

Chantel and I cracked up. That lady always brought everything back around to business.

"Ella, I've been around you and Hassan enough to know the man cares about you *and* is crazy about my nephew. He'll be able to handle how much or how little you decide to tell him."

"You're right." I dabbed at my moist eyes with a napkin. "Listen, I have to go pick up Zuri. She asked if she could talk to me about something."

Intrigued, Chantel pushed her plate with remnants of scrambled eggs and sausage to the side. She rested her elbow on the table. "Did she say what it was about?"

I shook my head. "Whatever it is, she doesn't want to talk to Hassan about it."

Mom grimaced, wrinkling her nose. "Oh, baby, that doesn't sound good."

"I know."

After putting my plate, mug, and silverware in the dishwasher, I hugged my mom and sister. "Tell sleepyhead Manny I'll be back later."

Seventeen

When I pulled up in front of Hassan's house on the other end of town bordering Jacksonville, Zuri and Kali were sitting on the front porch.

I couldn't resist taking my camera out of my tote bag and capturing candid shots of them. By now they were used to my antics. Zuri tapped her sister on the knee when she noticed me. They both made duck lips and posed, running their fingers down their box braids. Chantel and I had spent most of the day installing them last Saturday. I smiled remembering our time together. If we hadn't been watching movies, joking, and eating in between, the girls' hair wouldn't have taken all day and most of the night. Hassan and Manny grew tired of waiting for us to be done. They left us behind and went bowling and out to eat afterwards.

Hassan stepped out onto the porch with a white tank style ribbed shirt, red basketball shorts, and barefoot. He chuckled when I turned my attention to him, taking several shots.

Putting away my Nikon Z8, I climbed the five steps to the porch. Hassan grabbed my hand and pulled me to him for a kiss.

"I like what you've done with your hair. Reminds me of Alicia Keys back in the day."

Hassan reached out and glided his hand down one of my braids that fell just below my breasts. Our eyes held and connected when his knuckles unintentionally grazed my right breast, eliciting something deep in my core I hadn't felt since my college boyfriend who I would've probably married if I hadn't chosen my career. Settling down to marry and have babies wasn't part of my game plan.

"I guess me and Zuri better get going."

"Uh, Miss Ella...can Kali come with us too?"

Me and Hassan shared a look. I wondered if Zuri had told him what she wanted to speak with me about.

"Absolutely!"

We weren't going anywhere special. Just over to the studio for privacy. Later, I had to run over to my grandparents' house. Granddad X had agreed to let me go through Ilona's paintings to see which ones I wanted to hang in the gallery. My grandfather also said he had something to show me when I got there. I was excited to see what that something was. The box he had given me weeks ago was a few of Ilona's pottery pieces she had brought home with her from France. I had yet to decide if I was going to keep them for myself or display them in the gallery.

I didn't mind Kali coming along. I'd like to think Chantel and I were having a positive influence over them as sisters. Lately, I'd noticed the girls laughing and talking to each other more often than when they first arrived in Colemanville.

"Come on. Let's go!" I gave Hassan another kiss. As we reached the car he asked, "Do you mind if I take Manny over to Copper Lake to roller skate?

Zuri and Kali looked at each other before laughing. The last time we took the kids roller skating, my poor baby kept falling like an old drunk man. It was a good thing I insisted he wear a helmet, elbow and knee pads. Otherwise, he would've had scrapes and cuts everywhere.

I couldn't help laughing too. It was comical the way Manny's arms flailed about and the faces he made as he was trying not to go tumbling to the ground.

"Not at all. Please make sure he suits up in his gear."

Hassan gave me the thumbs up. "You got it, Mom."

We waved our goodbyes. Fifteen minutes later, we were walking through the doors of the gallery.

"I like it, Miss Ella." Kali turned in a slow circle before she gazed up at the tin ceiling. "Wow, that's cool."

"Come here. Let me show y'all something." I took them over to the wall where I had a copy of the original blueprint to the building in a black frame. "Your Dad's friend got the original blueprint from city hall and made me a copy."

Zuri leaned in to study the blueprint. "Wow! This building is over a hundred years old? How cool is that?"

"Pretty cool," Kali and I said at the same time. Before I could yell out, "jinx!", she beat me to it. The girls picked up saying "jinx" from me and Chantel. We tried being cool around the girls in an effort to relate to them. To show them we weren't old, boring adults. I supposed we were rubbing off on them with our back in the day slang.

I ushered them over to the tan leather sofa in the lounge area. Getting down to business, I looked directly at the girls. "What's going on?"

Zuri and Kali shared a dubious glance before the older sister spoke up.

"We don't want to go back home. Can you ask our dad if we can live with him?"

Wow...I hadn't seen that coming.

"May I ask why you want to live with your dad?"

Kali dropped her head. "You don't want us around?"

Seated between them, I wrapped my arms around Kali. "No, honey. That's not it. I just need to know so I can give your dad a reason."

What I said must've triggered the girls. At the sight of tears filling their eyes, my heart felt like it dropped to the pit of my stomach.

"I think we need to go talk to your dad...now."

Zuri jumped to her feet. "No! We're not supposed to tell."

Now I was triggered. Gently, I took Zuri's hand and pulled her down beside me. She laid her head on my shoulder when I wrapped my arm around her. The girls had mentioned their mother's boyfriend had moved in with them along with his teenaged son and daughter. When I spoke, it was slow and deliberate.

"When someone tells you not to say something, it's usually because what was said or done was a bad thing. It's okay to tell someone you trust...if what was said or done made you feel uncomfortable in *any* way." I looked from Zuri to Kali. "Understand?"

They both nodded, but remained silent for several seconds.

Hands in her lap, Zuri fidgeted with her fingers. "When my mom and her boyfriend aren't home, his kids have parties... They smoke weed and stuff. And they try to make us do it too."

Oh, God. I inhaled a slow, deep breath to calm my inner screaming, a technique I'd learned in counseling.

"How long are y'all alone with your mother's boyfriend's kids?"

Anger overwhelmed me from the terrified look in Kali's eyes. "My mom said not to tell my dad." She was now crying, wiping at her eyes.

Deep breath.

"Sometimes Mom and Mr. Darren go away for the weekend..." Zuri confessed.

"And they leave you and your sister alone with teenagers? Do they know the older kids are having parties? Getting high? And trying to make y'all get high?"

I knew my voice was escalating, but I couldn't help it. Nor could I help the myriad of horrible scenarios running haphazardly through my brain.

Kali said, "We told our mom. But she don't believe us because Mr. Darren said we were lying on his kids."

"But we weren't lying. Look." Zuri removed her cell phone from her back pocket. Her fingers trembled as she searched through her phone until she came to a video. She tapped the screen and handed me the phone.

Rowdy teens drinking alcohol and smoking weed with rap music blaring in the background were oblivious to being filmed. One of the teen boys yelled a sexually explicit comment. Stunned, my mouth hung open. "Who is that? And who is he talking to?"

My questions sent Kali into another fit of tears.

Zuri's eyes welled up. "Mr. Darren's son. He was talking to Kali."

Flashes of me on my apartment floor, pinned down, being violated played out in vivid color. Any second I was going to vomit.

"Did he ever touch either of you?"

The girls shook their heads.

"Are you sure?"

Zuri wiped her eyes with the back of her arm. "No, but I still don't like him. And we don't want to live there with them anymore. That's why I want you to ask our dad if we can live with him."

Lord, I had to help these babies. After what happened to me there was no way I wasn't going to insert myself in this matter.

"We can ask him together. Okay?"

Both girls nodded, a glimmer of hope in their dark eyes.

"This can't wait. I need to call your dad now."

Eighteen

"I know I'm getting on your nerves. But is there anything I can do for you, Hassan?" I'd asked that question almost a dozen times. He'd had yet to answer me.

I'd never forget the look of panic on his face when he arrived at the studio. That transformed from anguish to fury as the girls unfolded the hell they'd been forced, yes forced, to endure for the last year and a half. As minors, Zuri and Kali had no control over the adult decision their mother made to move in with a man and his children. I had never noticed the protruding vein in Hassan's forehead pulsating until I watched him looking at the video on Zuri's phone.

Immediately, Hassan had gotten his ex-wife on the phone to confront her. It didn't surprise me that she was defensive. What did surprise me was her defending her man's son's inappropriate sexual comment made to Kali, who was ten at the time. As a mother, I would've thought she'd be repulsed, livid.

Up until that point, Hassan's tone had been calm and even, almost menacing. It sent a chill down my spine because I sensed it was the peace before the storm. I could tell he was holding it together for the sake of his children. And then he snapped.

"What the hell do you mean that little punk only said he wanted to fuck my child because he was high? What the hell is wrong with you, Melinda?" Hassan roared.

Me and the girls jumped from Hassan's outburst. By their reaction, I knew that was the first time they'd witnessed their father that outraged.

I ushered the girls outside the gallery. It didn't do any good though. We could still hear Hassan yelling and pacing like a caged beast whose rage refused to be soothed. I had grabbed both girls by the hand and walked down the street to the end of the block, assuring them they'd done the right thing by coming to me. "Your father had to know what was going on in that house. None of this is your fault."

Fifteen minutes later, Hassan stepped outside and waved us back inside the gallery. I lost it when he held his girls in his arms, bathing them in his tears. At that moment I knew I wanted a future with Hassan.

Hassan took my hand and threaded our fingers before looking up into the stars from our perch on the top step of his front porch.

"Stop saying you're getting on my nerves. You being here with me is all I need." He kissed me on the forehead. "I'm grateful that my girls came to you before I put them on the plane to go back home." Hassan's nostrils flared upon drawing in a deep breath. "I didn't have a good feeling when Melinda told me she and the girls were moving in with Darren. I told her then if my daughters said one thing about anyone doing harm to them, I was coming to get them."

With his free hand, he rubbed the back of his neck. "I don't understand why they never said anything. I know I only see them twice a year but I talk to them almost every day on the phone. They never once said anything to me."

"It's not always easy to speak up," I whispered, trying to swallow the lump rising in my throat. "Because it's our nature to protect those we love by hiding the truth."

"Sounds like you're speaking from experience."

A tear splattered against our joined hands. "I am. That's why I called you right away."

I closed my eyes, shaking my head. "I would never want what happened to me to happen to Zuri or Kali."

Hassan's voice held tenderness when he spoke. "Baby, who hurt you?"

He held me as I trusted him with a huge chunk of my soul. My face between his hands, he dried my tears with his kisses, chasing the hurt and shame away. I never felt more cherished.

"I know you don't need me to take care of you and Manny. I want to because I care about and love you both. I want to protect both of you...keep you safe. Will you let me do that for you and Manny?"

That trepidation that held me prisoner every time I thought about how I was going to tell Hassan about Manny's conception no longer paralyzed me. I knew at some point I was going to have to divulge my past if I wanted a future with Hassan. Fear had held me captive, making me wonder what he would think of me. Would he blame me for being gullible to trust a man who'd expressed more than friendship? Or question me as to why I didn't sever the relationship when Preston stepped out of bounds that first time? I had asked myself that same question a thousand times.

Hassan had done none of those things. He held me and promised to protect me and my son. Manny wasn't an afterthought, but in the forefront of Hassan's mind. That was what pushed me over the cliff into a sea of love. I was grown enough to understand that sometimes life's circumstances changed things. Should our circumstances ever change, I would always love Hassan on the strength of his feelings for my son.

I turned my head to kiss the strong, yet tender hand that held my face. "Thank you for loving me, Hassan. I love you and the girls too. I *want* you to protect me and Manny. And I want to take care of and protect Zuri and Kali too."

For years I complained about my mother's overbearing ways. Never not once had I questioned her love for me and Chantel. Before the girls and Manny went inside to watch a movie, Zuri hugged me so tightly. "I wish you were our mother," she whispered in my ear.

Before I knew it, my heart responded, "So do I."

I wasn't a perfect parent. One thing I did pride myself on was being a fierce mama bear. Perfection couldn't eclipse that type of loyalty to a child.

"Kali is afraid her mother will make them come home."

"Not happening. I looked through Zuri's phone. She had another video with that punk and his friends saying all sorts of disgusting things to her and Kali. I sent them to Melinda and told her ass I was sending the videos to child protective services."

That's why he broke down earlier.

"What did she say?"

"Started crying and begging me not to report her." Hassan leaned forward to rest his forearms on his thighs and stared straight ahead. "I guess her job as an IT specialist with the government means more to her than her children. She was argumentative, defending her man and his son until I sent her those videos."

"Wow...I can't believe she wasn't the slightest outraged."

"I can. Her lack of interest in Zuri and Kali was the start to our failed marriage. They were nothing more than props for her to show off to her family and friends. She pretended she was the perfect mother when we'd have company or at holiday dinners. At home Melinda would get irritated with the girls for the slightest infraction. Ninety percent of our arguments were over how she treated our daughters. Over time we grew apart and she asked for a divorce. I wanted to take the girls. Out of spite she fought me in court for custody. The judge sided with her. The parent who literally provided over ninety-five percent of the care was granted one weekend a month, the summer, and two holidays a year. It didn't matter that Zuri and Kali wanted to be with me."

Taking in everything Hassan was sharing with me, it now made sense why Zuri was hostile toward me. The poor child probably feared me and Manny were going to be to Hassan what Darren and his kids had become to their mother, once again pushing her and Kali into the background.

"What are you going to do? Are you going to report her?"

I hope he doesn't give in to her.

"I told her she has one week to contact an attorney to sign over full custody. I'm also going to get counsel from Silas."

"Good idea." I covered my mouth to conceal a yawn. "Hassan, I would love to stay a little longer. But I'm exhausted and it's getting late."

He kissed my temple. "Don't go. I'll sleep on the couch. You and Manny can have my bed."

Although Hassan hadn't come right out and told me he needed me to be close to him tonight, I knew that was what he wanted. My growing love and affection for him wouldn't allow me to be anywhere else but here.

"Okay, we'll stay."

Hand in hand we stood and went inside. I didn't care what the neighbors would say.

Nineteen

"We're almost there guys."

I didn't have to turn around to see if the kids were uncomfortable in the backseat of the Mustang. The ride from church to my grandparents' home wasn't that far. Thank goodness, otherwise they'd be back there grumbling and elbowing each other.

"Yay! Drive faster, Daddy. Grandma Rose said she was making banana pudding for dessert. Hers is the best."

"Kali, I thought you said Grandma Rose's chocolate cake was the best? My favorite is her homemade strawberry ice cream."

Manny added his two cents. "Un-uhn, Grandma Rose's cookies are the best. I can eat them all day."

The girls giggled. "So can we!" they said in unison.

Hassan and I smiled at each other. We already knew whatever dessert Grandma Rose was serving, there would be enough for the children to take some home for later. I tried suggesting to my grandmother that it wasn't good for the kids to eat too many sweets. "You didn't have a problem eating up all the cakes and pies when you were a child," had been her sassy comeback, effectively shutting me up.

The girls adored Grandma Rose and Mom. I supposed because they fussed over them after learning about their ordeal under the care of their mother. Zuri and Kali were lavished with kisses to the forehead and embraces infused with grandmotherly love. When their mother, with her petty self, refused to send their clothes and keepsakes along with birth certificates, social security cards, and immunization records, Mom swooped in to the rescue. Boss lady in charge treated the girls to a weekend shopping spree in Atlanta for their back to school wardrobe. I thought she went a bit far when she treated them to the spa for massages.

As we pulled up in front of my grandparents' home, Chantel and Silas were on the sidewalk talking. I noticed my sister had her laptop tucked under her arm. Whatever conversation they were having seemed serious.

Eager to get inside, the kids were unbuckling their seatbelts before Hassan turned the engine off.

Manny leaned forward between the seats to eye Hassan. "We need a bigger car. I'm squished up back here all the time."

To Manny's grumbling, Zuri pulled him back and kissed him on the cheek. "At least we don't stink."

Hassan chuckled. "Your mom and I are working on it, Manny." He stepped out of the car to allow the kids out of the backseat.

"Y'all get inside and see if Grandma Rose needs any help."

They charged past Chantel and Silas, waving and saying hello.

I waited for Hassan to come around to the passenger side to open the door. I slid my hand into his when he reached for it to help me out of the vehicle. He pulled me to him, bringing our bodies dangerously close. I placed my hand on his solid chest and stared into his eyes. I wanted to finish what Manny had stated.

"Honey, we need to make a decision."

We hadn't told the kids we'd been looking for a SUV that would accommodate the five of us comfortably. There were two models we were going back and forth on.

He kissed the corner of my mouth. "We will. I promise."

Playfully, I rolled my eyes. "Yeah...yeah...promises, promises."

It didn't bother me to ride in separate vehicles for comfort's sake. Hassan, on the other hand, felt differently. If we were going out and it was local, he didn't see the point of us taking separate cars. For longer drives he was agreeable to separate vehicles. Secretly, I enjoyed being alone with the girls listening to music and chatting. I had a blast introducing them to music I listened to at their ages. Surprisingly, they liked Boyz II Men, EnVogue, Whitney Houston, TLC and other artists from that era. These special moments deepened our bond. Even after we had a vehicle to accommodate the five of us, I wasn't giving up my car time with the girls.

"Let's pick a day this week to go back to the dealership."

"Yes, let's do that, handsome," I sassed as we approached Chantel and Silas.

"Hey girl, why weren't you in church today? Late night?" I wiggled my eyebrows at my sister before giving both of them a hug. Chantel and Silas began dating shortly after he took me on as a client.

Hassan chuckled as he hugged Chantel and shook Silas' hand.

Last night Chantel had texted to let me know she was staying at Silas'. She had never done that before. I figured she needed time away from the kids *and* me. She was the auntie and sister of the century. Between meeting her work deadlines, looking after

Manny while I worked, and volunteering to help the girls decorate their rooms, she was knee deep in paint and fabric swatches, online searches for furniture and accessories to fit the girls' personalities. There wasn't much time for her to do anything for herself. I was happy she'd thought about herself and stayed with Silas.

"It was a late night. But not what you think."

Chantel's tone was far from the playfulness that was her brand. A glance at Silas' furrowed brow made me uncomfortable.

"We need to show you something. Anywhere private we can talk?" Silas asked.

I suggested we go upstairs to the guest room. Thankfully, everyone was in the kitchen busying themselves with preparing the afternoon meal as we quietly made our way upstairs. Chantel sat on the bed and patted the space beside her as she opened her laptop.

Hassan closed the door and stood beside me. Silas did the same with Chantel.

When Chantel slid the laptop over to me, Silas commented, "This is why Preston didn't show for court last week."

Surrounded by my family and Hassan for support, we waited two hours for Preston to show up in court for the trial. His attorney kept telling the judge his client was on his way. The judge was already way past frustrated with Preston's attorney's antics of postponing court dates. A bench warrant was issued against Preston.

I covered my mouth in horror. News clip after news clip played of Preston being arrested for the rape of a young woman who was an up and coming artist in New York. Photos of the badly beaten woman were flashed across the screen. Chantel clicked on another news site that showed four other women coming forward to accuse him of sexual assault. She clicked on another site of people in the streets of New York burning Preston's work.

When Chantel went to click on another site, I slammed the laptop shut. "I don't want to see anymore."

Hassan sat beside me and wrapped his arm around me. "Babe, you good?"

I blew out a breath. "I hate that this happened to those women. Maybe, if I had spoken up..."

Truth was, I'd been scared to speak up, too afraid of being called a liar or labeled a scorned lover even though Preston and I never had an intimate relationship. The prospect of Preston and Victoria further tarnishing my name in the art community and destroying my family's legacy and bringing shame to my great-grandmother Ilona's name silenced me. After all, who would believe a woman who didn't abort a pregnancy although I had the legal right to do so if I wanted?

"No, the hell you don't, Ella! Don't you dare go feeling guilty about this. This is on Preston. Not you!"

Hassan kissed my temple. "Your sister is right, babe. Don't do this to yourself. You had enough you were dealing with at the time."

"Doesn't mean I can't speak up now." I looked at my attorney. "Right?"

"Absolutely. Right now, Preston is denying the allegations and claiming all his relationships were consensual. He even has previous women he dated coming to his defense." Silas fell silent and drew in a deep breath. "I have a friend from law school who works in the district attorney's office. Those four women in the news clip reporting Preston over a year ago sparked an investigation into the allegations. I can't prove it. But that's probably why he tried to kidnap Manny. Apparently, there was a leak and Preston got wind of the investigation. Who knows?" Silas hunched his shoulders. "His motive for trying to kidnap your son could've been to keep you silent."

That was when I broke down. A primal wail released from the pit of my soul. "I hate him! I hate him! I hate him…" was the litany I screamed until my voice was hoarse.

My parents came barging in the room. I could hear my mother telling the girls to take Manny in the backyard. Seconds later, my grandparents entered.

"What is going on?" Mom inquired hysterically, rushing over to kneel in front of me.

Chantel and Silas took turns bringing my parents and grandparents up to speed. Hassan held and rocked me, soothing my agitated spirit.

"I'm an old man. I've lived my life. I swear to God and all the angels in heaven if that no good for nothing steps foot in Colemanville I again…he's gonna wake up in hell."

When I looked up at Granddad X, tears were in his eyes. My father's hand was resting on his shoulder. "If I don't get to him first, Dad."

Hassan shook his head. "Naw, death is too good for a punk like him. He needs to be beaten within an inch of his life."

I appreciated and loved my family. But I had enough of the violent rhetoric.

"Please, y'all stop. We need to be smart about this. I agree Preston needs to be held accountable. But not like how y'all are talking about."

I looked at my dad and grandfather. "Do you think I'd be able to go on knowing y'all would end up in prison? At your age?" Turning to Hassan, I cupped his tense jaw. "You're the best thing that's come into my life in a long time. Do you think I want to lose you for beating the crap out of Preston? What about our girls? Honey, they need you. Me and Manny need you."

Hassan let out a deep breath before kissing the palm of my hand. "You're right, babe."

"Ella, are you sure you want to get involved?" Silas inquired.

I didn't have to think long to give my answer. This thing was bigger than me. If my voice, in some small way, could bring justice to myself and the other women, I had to speak up.

"I'm all in."

Twenty

Knots intertwined in my stomach caused me to have mild cramping. For the last two hours I'd sat in Silas' office with Chantel and Hassan at my side as I recounted my history with Preston via a Zoom meeting.

The District Attorney, Jasmine Abrams, was a sister with a fade cut and stylish wire framed glasses. She made me feel comfortable with the difficult questions she asked about my relationship with Preston. I was warned to be prepared for Preston's legal team to drag me through the mud if called to testify in court. If the case went that far. Ms. Abrams did give me a glimmer of hope. Preston could take a plea deal which would save me from having to testify.

It was disgusting that he had a group of supporters behind him calling his victims liars. Photos of Preston with the women positioned in what appeared to be intimate poses were all over the blogs and television. I knew firsthand how Preston manipulated those photos to give the illusion that more than business was going on. Or even to suggest the women were enamored with the great Preston Jennings. Flashes of him at my side during the opening night of my exhibit, ready to pull me to his side for a photo op, infuriated me. *Sneaky bastard.* I was being set up and hadn't realized it until the aftermath. Chantel and I had a long conversation wondering if I'd been his first victim or had there been others before me? I didn't doubt it since he was almost a decade older than me.

Two weeks prior to our zoom meeting I had FedExed photocopies of my journals to District Attorney Abrams. It devastated me that I had to expose the darkest period of my life and the years following to present day. Everything was chronologized from our meeting and his unsolicited offer to help me exhibit my work that led to the assault. His popping in and out of my life. Manny's aversion to him. Victoria's admission to him stalking me and breaking into my home, stealing me and Manny's passports. And his arrest for attempting to kidnap Manny was emotionally penned. What the photocopies hadn't revealed were the tear soaked pages.

"Ms. Caswell, your journal will definitely be a crucial part of our evidence. The details in which you describe the events are in sync with the testimonies of the other victims. It demonstrates Mr. Jennings has been a sexual predator for years. His pattern is the same. Meets and befriends a beautiful young artist, attempts a *consensual* relationship, when that doesn't work he offers to mentor and help advance her in the art community. When he gets tired of the chase, he takes what he's been after all along."

Wow. The man had a playbook. It infuriated me how he used me and the other women as pawns in his sick, twisted game. I wasn't alone. Chantel's heavy sigh and Hassan's low growl told me as much.

"I'm glad they'll be useful. I just want to do my part to speak up so that we all hopefully get justice." With the way our justice system could be at times, all I had was hope.

"Thank you for coming forward. I understand it must've been a difficult decision."

After Chantel showed me those videos, I had to come forward. Uncomfortable, yes. Difficult, no.

My tribe was standing beside me, holding me up and fortifying me. I could face the monster and his supporting minions. My only concern was keeping Manny protected from the fallout this could cause. Ms. Abrams gave me her word that if at all possible, she would protect my identity. But couldn't promise it wouldn't get leaked once Preston's legal team learned I had come forward. I wasn't asking for monetary damages like the other women. Ms. Abrams said this might keep the other side in check.

After the meeting ended, I let out a huge sigh of relief.

"That wasn't so bad. Let's go have a celebratory lunch."

School was back in. There was plenty of time for us to grab lunch before the kids would be home.

Hassan grabbed me in a bear hug. "I'm so proud of you, babe. I love you."

Chantel and Silas echoed my man's sentiment. Well...not the I love you part from Silas. All the same it made me feel incredibly supported and cared for. I kissed Hassan tenderly. "I love you, too."

"Where do you want to go for lunch?"

I grinned at Hassan and before I could open my mouth, he knew where I wanted to go. To that quaint bistro in downtown Jacksonville where I had taken him to lunch that pretty much propelled us into a relationship. It was our getaway spot when we left the kids with my parents to have a few hours of alone time. With all of the chaos going on, Hassan and I hadn't gotten around to our overnight getaway. The time had never seemed quite right. And with his girls living with him permanently, I didn't want to bring it up.

"To our spot." Jokingly he said, "You sure you want to let these two in on our little piece of paradise?"

A few hours alone holding hands, eating sandwiches, and

drinking sweet tea was paradise to him. I really loved that man and how beautiful and simple our lives were together.

Tapping my chin with my finger, I tilted my head toward the ceiling. Chantel nudged me with her elbow. "Girl, stop thinking so hard."

We all laughed.

"You'll forever be my bratty little sister."

"Yep. Now come on, I'm starving."

It took us no time to get to the bistro. The place was crowded. We didn't mind waiting out front on the bench for our table to be ready. Hassan and Silas were having a lively, trash talking discussion about football and predicting which team was going to make it to the Super Bowl when my business phone rang. Business was picking up. I was getting at least two to three calls a day to do Halloween photoshoots, mostly families with small children. Though I didn't celebrate the holiday, I did get a kick out of the costumes the families would come to the studio dressed in.

I excused myself to walk a few feet away to take the call which wouldn't take long because I always referred clients back to the website to complete the intake form.

"Ella Caswell. How can I help you?"

"You bitch!"

Over Preston calling me every foul name and accusing me of trying to ruin him, I matched his outrage.

"You're sick, Preston! This is on you. Why don't you do me a favor and go somewhere and drop dead?"

He knew he wasn't supposed to have any contact with me or my son. And had no business calling, emailing, or texting me. You best believe I was reporting him for violating the protective order.

With lightning speed Hassan was at my side taking the phone. The Hassan that showed up when he confronted his ex-wife made an appearance. Chantel and Silas rushed over.

He wasn't shouting. His tone was even, menacing.

"Let this be the last time you call my woman's number..."

Preston must've been pumped up on a drug or something. I couldn't make out what he was saying. Whatever he just said brought a sinister smirk to Hassan's full lips. Was I crazy? Or was my man looking *extra* sexy? Being all chivalrous and everything over me. Chantel must've seen it too.

"Girl, you better go on that overnight trip."

Though I agreed, I hushed her so I wouldn't miss anything.

"You ain't said nothing but a word, punk... You know where to find me. The next time I see you I'mma break your back in half."

Hassan ended the call. "Stupid motha..." He held back from completing the expletive in front of me and Chantel. If I had to guess it was because he expressed feeling horrible when he dropped the F bomb in front of me and the girls.

"Dammmn! Bruh, I didn't know you had it in you," Silas said, half serious, half joking.

"I know! Right?" Chantel playful slapped Silas on the chest. "You better defend my honor like that, Silas."

As angry as Hassan was, he chuckled, pulling me into a protective embrace.

"No doubt I'm gonna defend my baby. Every day. All day."

I melted into Hassan, soaking up everything he was infusing into me. The words that rolled out of me came as naturally as the air I breathed.

"One of the *many* reasons why I love you."

"Love you too, babe."

Hassan reached for his vibrating phone. "Our table is ready."

After we were seated and served water, Silas stated the obvious.

"There's a snake in the DA's office. No way Preston called you so quickly after our meeting with Abrams. Did he mention anything about the journals?"

"No, he didn't. Just that I had spoken with the DA."

Hassan rested his arm against the back of my chair. "Yeah, someone in there is talking. Silas, is there any way you can find out what's going on?"

"Can't promise anything, but I'm definitely reaching out to Abrams when I get back to the office. She needs to know her office is compromised."

Silas looked me in the eyes. I always knew he was kind, but there was something extra about the way he was looking at me, like we were family. He and Chantel were now an official item. Maybe that was why he cared.

"Are you okay, Ella? If you want to back out..." He looked at Hassan and Chantel. "We'll understand. Dude is losing it. He knows you coming forward is going to strengthen the case against him."

"I'm good, Silas. And committed to following this through. I can't be...I won't be silent this time."

"Bastard knows he's done," Chantel commented before taking a sip from her glass of water. "I just hate that..."

An awkward silence filled the space. We all knew what my sister was going to say. I'd said it a million times to myself. And then I would look at my baby and see how precious and innocent he was in a world of ugliness. I stopped questioning God why the Plan B hadn't worked for me that one time when it had worked during my college years.

"I'm Manny's father. Period."

The set determination in Hassan's jawline left no room for me to doubt his sincerity. Overwhelmed, all I could do was lean into him, burying my face in his chest. Silent tears released gratitude. I was incapable of forming coherent words to express myself.

I reached for a napkin to dry my tears. That didn't do any good because more tears came when I saw that Chantel was crying too. My confidant, I had poured my heart out to her about my concerns for Manny not having a father. She knew my fears of being inadequate to teach him the things about being a man. It wasn't that I was of the mindset that a woman couldn't raise a boy child to be an astounding man. Women had been doing it for centuries. But that didn't mean I didn't want my son to benefit from the love and guidance of a father.

Of course, my dad and grandfather had always been there, doing things with Manny since he was born. I appreciated both of them for being father figures to my baby. But I wanted more for Manny. He deserved to have a man be present in his life from the moment he opened his beautiful eyes in the morning until he laid his head down at night. Was that too much for me to ask for?

Hassan kissed my temple. "You hear what I'm saying to you?" he murmured for my ears only. The thick emotion in his voice made me love him even more. I not only heard him. Every ounce of my being believed him.

"Yes."

"Good. Let's order our food and do what we came here to do."

Chantel waved the server over who had been lingering on the periphery.

"Yes! To celebrate my amazing sister. My new shero."

Dramatically, I threw my hand to my chest. "New! I thought I was always your shero."

"Girl, you know what I mean."

We didn't give Preston or his call any more energy. Silas vowed to contact Ms. Abrams to make her aware of Preston's call. I was paying him a decent amount of money to do his job. So that was what I was going to do. Let my attorney handle it. Other pressing things required my attention.

Our conversation turned to my upcoming exhibit scheduled for the second Friday in November. Invitations had gone out two weeks ago to the residents and business owners of Colemanville, friends, and former colleagues. Mom had invited her business contacts in the neighboring towns. RSVPs were coming in and I was ecstatic mixed with a tinge of apprehensiveness. In the back of my mind, I was fretting over if there would be a decent turnout.

I necessarily wasn't a perfectionist. But I wanted Miss Iva Rae's portrait to be perfect for Jillian. There were minor touch ups I wanted to do. Initially, I was going to wait until Jillian's grand opening of her day spa to give her the portrait. Mom suggested I present it to my childhood friend at the exhibit. "It'll be a plug for Jillian's business. And show outsiders Colemanville's legacy of women doing great things."

After we were done, Hassan and Silas split the bill after haggling over who was going to pay for lunch. Before parting, Chantel agreed to pick Manny up from school. We weren't comfortable with Manny walking home with Zuri and Kali just yet. Besides, the girls had met friends that they walked home with after school. I remembered being that age. The last thing I would've wanted was a seven-year-old tagging along while I talked girl stuff with my friends.

Chantel and I hugged. "I'll be home soon. I have to stop by the old folks' house. Granddad X wants to give me something."

"Alright. Take your time. I'll make sure the kids do their homework and get dinner started."

I hugged my sister again. "You're the real shero," I whispered in her ear.

Twenty-One

"When you gonna marry my granddaughter?" Grandma Rose inquired from her rocking chair as Hassan and I stepped on the porch holding hands.

Hassan chuckled, getting a kick out of my grandmother. In private he called her undercover spicy grandma because of her on the whim line of direct questioning. "The lady don't pull no punches."

My face flushed and I felt hot all over. Every Sunday afternoon, my grandmother dropped hints about the direction of where our relationship was heading. I tried gently telling her a time or two that we hadn't discussed taking that step as of yet. Today, I supposed she was coming right out with it. Like always, my grandfather saved the day.

"Rose, leave that man alone. You can't rush a man into a life altering situation."

Grandma Rose leaned forward, squaring her shoulders, raring with a comeback when Hassan cut her off.

"I'm working on it, Miss Rose."

My grandmother was something else. She leaned back,

tilted her head, and stared Hassan straight in the eye. "Young man, I need you to work a little faster. Ella needs a husband to keep her warm at night. Manny needs a daddy."

Oh, now I was really embarrassed. "Grandma Rose!"

Hassan was really laughing now. I elbowed him into silence. He whispered in my ear, "Spicy."

I elbowed him again, refusing to laugh.

Granddad X stood, shaking his head. "Everybody thinks your grandmother is this sweet, genteel lady...and she is. But she can be just as meddlesome as she wants to be."

Hassan and I looked to Grandma Rose for a witty retort. We waited. But she didn't say a word. Before she went back to rocking, she rolled her eyes at my grandfather.

"Come on, Ella. Let me show you what I got for you."

"Okay." I released Hassan's hand to kiss Grandma Rose on the cheek. "Don't pay Granddad X any mind."

"I ain't worried about that man. He's being fresh 'cause you and Hassan are here."

Shuffling to the door, Granddad X grunted, "You coming in, young man?'

"No, sir. I'm gonna sit out here with Grandma Rose." Hassan eased down on the swing across from Grandma Rose's rocker, asking her about her day as Granddad X and I entered the house.

Inside on the dining room table sat a beautiful wooden carved box. As I got closer, a vibrant jewel green, blue, and fuchsia hummingbird in flight painted on the lid drew my attention. From its craftsmanship, I could tell it was a vintage piece. Delicately, I ran my hand over the lacquer finish that had preserved the colors over the years. I gazed up at my grandfather.

"Belonged to my mama. She and Daddy made it as a high school project. Daddy did the carving and Mama the painting."

Granddad X's arthritic finger pointed to the precious treasure. "Mama loved hummingbirds. Said they were the most beautiful birds God created."

"Wow."

I picked the box up to better inspect its intricate details. The hinges that allowed the box to open and close were an ornate copper. My fingers traced the decorative carvings as I studied the piece of art created by two people whose blood flowed through my veins. Two people who loved each other so much that the other couldn't exist without them. Anyone would be blessed to experience that kind of love.

"This is beautiful, Granddad X. Is there anything inside?"

His grin was lopsided. "Open it and see."

Giddily, I lifted the lid. My eyes misted as I stared at the carving of the initials I.R. + G.T. encased in a heart on the inside of the lid. Dozens of black and white photos were inside along with an envelope that had to be older than my granddad from its brownish-yellow hue. Old photos intrigued me. I would imagine by the expressions on the faces of the people in them what they were thinking. Were they sad? Happy? Peeved? For some reason, the face down envelope called to me the loudest. When I picked it up and flipped it over, my heart skipped. In the upper left side, written in bold script, was Nubian-Kush Collaborative with the rest of the address. Ilona's name was on the center of the envelope.

"Oh my God," I breathed out. Gingerly, I removed the letter and read it silently. When I was done, I glanced up at my grandfather.

"This is your mother's acceptance letter to present her work."

I could tell Granddad X was overcome with emotion by his quivering bottom lip. He nodded his response.

After several seconds, he found his voice. "I think Mama would want you to have this too."

I hadn't noticed the painting leaning against the wall. He picked it up and brought it over to the side of the table where I was standing holding the letter. Carefully placing the painting on the table in front of me, he held it up. A golden brown woman was standing barefoot in a field of vibrant green grass and a variation of bright colorful flowers with her face toward the sun. A sublime smile curved her full lips. You could almost feel the cool breeze causing the ends of her white flowy dress to lift and the massive shoulder length curls blowing in the wind.

"This is stunning." I'd seen enough of Ilona's work to know she always put the title and date of her paintings on the back of the canvas. "Granddad X, turn it around please."

Graceful Watercolors, nineteen forty-nine was etched in the corner.

"You know what's interesting about this painting?" I didn't wait for my grandfather to respond. I answered my own question. "For your mom to have painted this in nineteen forty-nine the hair on the woman is contemporary. Black women weren't wearing their hair like this back then." I'd seen enough old photos, magazines, and race movies to know what I was talking about. So did my grandfather.

"Mama said she would sometimes get visions of what she was going to paint."

What Granddad X said next sent chills through me.

"I believe this is you, Ella, in the painting. Look at the skin tone and hair...the woman in the painting has on those bracelets you're wearing."

I couldn't deny the hair and skin observation. My gaze went to the three gold bangle bracelets I wore every day. The woman in the painting wore three bracelets too. In awe, I whispered, "You think so?"

Granddad X nodded, taking the painting and placing it against the wall. "I sure do."

Captivated, I needed my grandfather to tell me more. "What do you think it means?"

"I suppose that you would find God's grace in your life when you needed it the most. What do you think of this one?"

He held a painting of a man and woman in an intimate embrace on a bed tangled in sheets. Their nudity was tastefully concealed. This painting, with its sensual message, intrigued me. I took the painting from my grandfather's hand to study it. I'd seen dozens of my great-grandmother's paintings. But nothing ever this passionate.

"This one is so different from the other paintings."

"That's because Mama also painted using a different name. None of us knew until after her death. Was something she and Daddy kept to themselves."

He pointed to the signature at the bottom right corner of the painting. Enraptured with the painting I hadn't noticed the artist's signature.

"What? LoLo Rivers! LoLo Rivers was my great-grandmother?! Oh, I gotta call Chantel."

My grandfather was tickled by my enthusiasm. As I was dialing, I gushed, "You don't understand how big this is, Granddad X. Two of her paintings are in a museum in Nice, France."

I didn't give Chantel a chance to say anything. "Girl, you have to come to Granddad X and Grandma Rose's like now. Hurry! Drive safe."

Fifteen minutes later Chantel and Hassan entered the living room.

"Where are the kids?"

"On the porch with Grandma Rose. Why did I have to rush over here? I was about to fix dinner."

I did a little dance. "Dinner can wait. This is better." I held the LoLo Rivers painting up and pointed to the signature.

"Oh. My. Goodness! A LoLo Rivers painting. It's gorgeous. Let me see."

Chantel took the painting from me and held it at different angles, examining it as if she was authenticating it. She stared at our grandfather with a look of disbelief.

"Where'd you get this painting from Granddad X?"

I squeezed Chantel's forearm. "Girl, LoLo Rivers was Ilona."

Gazing at the painting as if looking in a mirror, it took several seconds for what I'd said to register in Chantel's brain.

"Wait a minute...what?" Her voice hitched a higher octave. "Are you for real?!"

Her gaze shot over to our grandfather for confirmation. "Is Ella for real? As in our great-grandmother, Ilona Robertson-Thurman?"

"Yes, ma'am. I got several more LoLo Rivers paintings in storage. I'll give you one. I'm sure your Mama would want one too."

My impatient inner child was screaming for Granddad X to go across town to his storage container and get those paintings right now! The one Chantel held was titled *The Marriage Bed*. I wondered if the others were as tastefully provocative?

"This beauty along with *Graceful Watercolors* are going in the gallery."

To pay homage to my great-grandmother, I'd dedicated an area of the gallery to showcase her work. It was my desire that everyone who walked through the doors of my gallery experienced the beauty of her work.

"Babe, we're going to need to beef up the security system at the gallery. I'm no art expert, but I'm guessing if your great-grandmother's paintings are in a museum in France, they're pretty valuable."

"For sure," Chantel agreed before asking to see *Graceful Watercolors*.

When our grandfather held the painting up on the table, Hassan and Chantel gave each other an eerie look. "Ella, *that* is you in the painting. This is kinda spooky."

Hassan shook his head. "Nah, not so, Chantel. More like Miss Ilona had a special gift that went beyond being an exceptional artist."

"Yes, sir. Mama was gifted indeed." Granddad X nodded toward me and Chantel. "Passed the gift on to Ella and Chantel."

Chantel and I linked arms, our smiles saturated in pride. Not too many nights ago, after Manny was in bed and Hassan and the girls had gone home, we grabbed a bottle of wine and snacks. On the back patio, under the dark, velvet sky and stars, we talked for hours about how coming back to Colemanville, a place we couldn't wait to leave as teenagers, was the best move we'd made in years. A little older and wiser, we appreciated the intimacy of small town living. It wasn't so bad that your neighbors were aware of your comings and goings. If my neighbor Mrs. Winter hadn't called the police when she noticed Preston circling the block looking at my house, Manny could be in another country right now.

Somehow our conversation turned to Ilona. "Ella, do you ever wonder why out of Ilona and Gabe's grandchildren and great-grandchildren me, you, and Jasper are the only ones who are artists?"

I had never given it much thought. Most likely because my great aunts and uncle were successful professionals in their fields.

"I don't know. Maybe because we were exposed to her work the most. Well...not so much Jasper. He takes after Gabe."

Out of our grandfather's siblings, he was the only one who stayed in Colemanville. The others migrated to larger cities in the south. Once Ilona and Gabe passed on, Granddad X's siblings, their children, and grandchildren only came back to Colemanville for special occasions. We would travel to visit Granddad X's siblings and their families too. Ilona's work was proudly on display in their homes too. But not like my grandparents' home. Literally, every room showcased a piece of Ilona's art. Whether it was a painting or a photograph, Ilona's presence was there.

"Probably... Do you think she would be proud of us?"

"I don't see why not. You're an amazing graphic artist with a big shot advertising agency. And my photography business has been thriving for years. I'd say Ilona and Gabe are smiling down on us."

Reminiscing on that late night talk with my sister, I had to remind our grandfather that he was gifted too. "Granddad X, what about you? Your mama taught you everything about photography."

Granddad X was Colemanville's unofficial resident photographer, always snapping photos at town events.

"*And* your daddy taught you how to design and make furniture," Chantel chimed in.

Great-granddad Gabe was truly extraordinary. He hadn't let losing part of his right arm in World War II diminish him as a man. From what I'd been told by family, he worked twice as hard as any man and was three times as strong. Though I was a young child when he passed away, prior to his passing, I have vague memories of me and Chantel sitting between him and Ilona on the swing on my grandparents' front porch.

"My aunt and uncle said people would come from all over to buy from Thurman's Fine Furniture. When I moved to Colemanville before they passed away, they gifted me with nightstands from your showroom."

Folks still traveled a distance to purchase one of a kind furniture.

Chest stuck out, pride illuminated Granddad X's weathered features. He took his furniture making skills seriously. Even though he was up in age, a sketch pad was never far from reach for him to doodle an inspiration when it hit him. Retirement didn't stop him from popping in and out of the store his great-grandfather had opened in the late eighteen hundreds to check in on my second cousin, Granddad X's nephew, Jasper Thurman. Jasper was blessed with the carpentry gene. After obtaining his MBA, he and his family moved to Colemanville to run the business. Under Jasper's management, Thurman's Fine Furniture remained in good financial standing.

"Are my initials carved in the top drawer? If not..." Granddad X waved his hand in the air, almost in disgust. "It's one of those copycats."

"Copycat?" Chantel and I said in unison, amused by our grandfather's terse remark.

As far as we knew, skilled carpenters worked with our family to create furniture. Pieces weren't mass produced.

"If a Thurman didn't make it, it's a copycat. My Daddy told me when these two hands..." Granddad X held up his hands for emphasis. "Created something beautiful out of what was once much of nothing to be proud of. To put my mark on it. Every Thurman that created a piece of furniture carved their initials in it."

Every now and then, Granddad X's resentment flared to the surface over an incident that happened decades ago. As business grew Granddad X had to rely on outside carpenters to assist with making furniture. A carpenter he'd hired and trusted like a family member attempted to overtake the business. Granddad X nor Grandma Rose never divulged what went down. All I knew was that my grandfather had worked past retirement age until Jasper stepped in to take over the business.

Hassan listened intently as Granddad X retold the story, leaving out details of the event that led to backstabbing.

"If a Thurman didn't make it. It's a copycat."

"Miss Ella..."

I turned to see Kali clutching her stomach. "Can we leave? I don't feel good."

"Of course, sweetheart."

Hassan went over to her and placed the back of his hand against her forehead.

"Go on and take that precious baby home," Granddad X commanded as he took the painting from Chantel and propped it against the wall. "I'll bring these over to the gallery when you update your alarm system. Now take that baby home."

Twenty-Two

By the time we arrived at my house, Kali was doubled over and crying. Hassan carried her to the bathroom where he left us alone. As I suspected, she had gotten her first period. In the linen closet where I kept pads, I took one out and showed her how to place it in her underwear before putting her in my bed. Chantel brought me the hot water bottle Grandma Rose told her to get from the top shelf in the bathroom closet before we'd left our grandparents.

"Here sweetie, put this on your stomach."

Kali's voice was small and doubtful. "What is it?"

Tenderly, I stroked her cheek as I sat beside her on the bed. "It's a hot water bottle. Women use it when they get their period to help soothe the cramps."

It didn't seem all that long ago when my mother placed this same hot water bottle on my belly to rid me of terrible cramps.

"I don't want to be a woman." A single tear slid down Kali's cheek.

"Aww, sweetie. It's not that you're exactly a woman. But your body is preparing to become a woman."

I wanted to ask her so bad if her mother had prepared her by giving her the birds and the bees talk.

"How?"

Nope, she hadn't.

"When young girls get their periods, it's a sign that her body can carry a baby."

Kali shot up. Her eyes went wild. "A baby?!"

Gently, I nudged her shoulder to get her to lie back down.

"Yes, but some other things have to take place before a girl or woman can have a baby. Don't worry. You're not going to have a baby. When you're feeling better, either your dad or I will talk to you about nature. I'm going to go fix you a sandwich and get you a Motrin to take to help with the cramps too."

"Okay."

Halfway to the door, Kali called out, "Thank you for letting me come to your house, Miss Ella."

"You're welcome, sweetie. I'll be right back."

I PLOPPED down on the sofa beside Hassan. When I got back upstairs with Kali's food and pain medication, she had drifted off to sleep. I didn't want to disturb her, so I left her sleeping.

"Where's Chantel and the kids?"

"She took them to the dairy for ice cream after they ate dinner." His somber tone didn't go unnoticed.

"You okay?"

Hassan was headed in the direction of his home when Kali asked if she could go home with me. Though he hadn't questioned her request, I could tell he wanted to take his daughter home to take care of her.

"My baby is growing up on me... Too fast. Before you know it, she'll be headed off to college."

I rubbed his thigh. "Let's not think that far ahead."

Stretching out his legs, Hassan folded his hands behind his head. "I knew this day would come..." He turned his head to gaze at me. "Just wished it hadn't come so fast. I'm still adjusting to them being with me full-time. And enjoying learning little things about them."

The hint of Hassan's smile made me feel all warm inside. "Like what?"

"Zuri comes off like she's the bossy one. But low key, it's Kali. Kali's more diplomatic with her bossiness. And she's a neat freak. Zuri tries to act like she's tough and aloof. She's not though. That girl is a big softie."

Laughing, I had to agree.

"Kali's bossiness is paying off around here. I can't tell you how much I have to fuss at Manny to straighten up his room. The other day I walked past his room and she was in there, angelic as ever, getting Manny to clean up." I imitated Kali's squeaky voice. "Manny, put your shoes in the closet so we can watch cartoons. And pick up your clothes off the floor so Mommy doesn't have to fuss at you."

"Is that right?"

"Mmmm-hmmm. And Manny listened to her."

"What about Zuri?"

Hassan chuckled when I groaned. "Lord, I thought Zuri was going to run me away. That little girl did not like me." I grabbed Hassan's hand. "Now every time she sees me, she gives me a hug. Hassan, I love your girls."

"I'm still stuck on Kali calling you Mommy."

Every muscle in my face was activated when I smiled. "I know. She hasn't come right out and called me that. A couple times she slipped up and corrected herself."

"Would you have a problem if she did?"

"Honestly...yes and no."

Hassan sat up, disengaging our hands. "Explain."

"My heart already loves Zuri and Kali. I know I would be a great mom to them."

I stared Hassan in his eyes so he understood that I was sincere. "But I would need more of a commitment from you... from me."

My traditional upbringing had me thinking a lot lately about our situation. I knew Hassan loved me and I loved him but I was getting to the place where I desired permanency in our relationship. Not just for us, but for our children too.

That lopsided grin of his that I loved so much curved his full lips. "Ella Caswell, are you proposing to me in a roundabout way?"

I threw my head back and cracked up. "It did sound like one, didn't it?" My comfort level with this man wouldn't allow me to be embarrassed.

Large hands framed my face. "I'd take you to the courthouse tomorrow morning and marry you if I didn't think your parents and grandparents would have my hide."

"Is that a proposal, Mr. Murphy?"

His kiss was long and passionate. It took everything in me not to straddle him right there in my living room.

"It's the prelude to the proposal."

Twenty-Three

Giddily, I jogged the short distance from the kitchen to the front door. My heart was fluttering and there wasn't a doggone thing I could do about it. On the other side of the door Hassan stood there with an overnight bag. Today he wore a gray T-shirt with his company's logo, jeans, and black work boots. I pulled him in by the front of his shirt and kissed him.

"Good morning," I whispered against his mouth. He tasted like wintergreen mint and smelled clean and masculine like sandalwood and patchouli.

"Where are the kids?"

Though it was a school night, Hassan allowed the girls to stay over. Before he left last night, I asked his permission to talk to the girls about womanly things. He had given his blessing and thanked me for saving him from having to do it himself.

"Just woke them up. They're getting ready for school."

"Good."

His arm snaked around my waist to draw me in closer for a lingering kiss brimming on the edge of eroticism. It was a good thing I had woken up early to shower and do my morning routine before Hassan showed up with the girls' change of clothes.

I let out a dreamy sigh when he leaned down to bury his nose in the crook of my neck.

"You smell pretty."

Giggling, I thanked him and led him by the hand into the kitchen where I had begun to start breakfast.

"Have a seat, mister."

Hassan slid onto a chair at the kitchen table as I went back to whipping up eggs. Last night Chantel had prepped the batter for the Belgian waffles.

"What are you making?"

I glanced over my shoulder to smile at him. "Your favorites. Waffles, cheesy scrambled eggs, and country ham."

He sank his teeth into his bottom lip. "Woman, you're talking my love language."

"Hey, Daddy."

Hassan kissed his eldest on the forehead. "Morning, Zuri. You and your sister's clothes are in the overnight bag on the sofa."

"Okay."

Zuri came over to me and wrapped her arms around my waist, kissing me on the cheek.

"Morning, Miss...Mom."

The girls shared with me and Chantel last night what it was like living with their mother, her man, and his kids. They both expressed how they felt their existence was an inconvenience in that household. What broke my heart, and I could tell Chantel felt the same, was how their mom would pit the girls against each other. Criticizing Kali because of her weight and thick, coarse hair. "She would always say I look just like my dad and have his nappy hair," Kali had whispered. Kali looked at her sister. "She would say Zuri was pretty like her."

My heart bled for poor Zuri as she apologized to her sister.

Chantel had held Kali as I held Zuri, tears cleansing and healing their young wounds. It wasn't my place to judge another woman's parenting skills. But it didn't prevent me from knowing that those girls hadn't been nurtured. I nor my sister could deny them when they asked if they could call us Mom and Auntie.

"Morning, baby. Take your clothes upstairs so you and your sister can get dressed. Don't want you to be late for school. Your dad might not let you stay over again on a school night."

Zuri's grin matched the bright sun rays streaming through the windows.

"Yes, ma'am."

Upon hearing her footsteps going upstairs, Hassan asked, "Did I miss something?"

Quickly, I gave Hassan a rundown of what the girls had shared. The pained expression on his face made me go to him. I stood behind him, massaging his tense shoulders.

"I wish I could wring her neck," he grumbled.

"What good would it do?"

Taking my hand, he brought me around to sit on his lap. He laid his head on my shoulder

"Nothing," he breathed out.

"Exactly."

We were in the middle of a tender kiss when Manny came charging down the steps yelling for me.

"Mommy! Mommy! Are you Zuri and Kali's mommy now?"

He skidded to a stop with his toothbrush in hand upon seeing Hassan. Thank goodness I had a split second to hop off of Hassan's lap.

Manny's inquisitive gazed volleyed between me and

Hassan as he waited expectantly for me to respond. Instead of answering, I asked a question of my own.

"Would you like that, Manny? If I was Zuri and Kali's mommy?"

His head bobbed up and down. "Then Mr. Hassan could be my daddy too."

My eyes stung, tears building. Hassan had that same look in his eyes that afternoon when he carried Manny to the guest room at my grandparents' home. Then I didn't want to believe what my heart was feeling. I thought my eyes were playing tricks on me. But they weren't. Hassan's reaction toward my son from the beginning had been paternal without having any rhyme or reason, as if it was a natural occurrence.

Hassan held his hand out to Manny. When Manny stepped in front of Hassan, he lovingly rested his hands on Manny's shoulders.

"Manny, I am your daddy. Don't let anyone tell you any different. You hear me?"

Staring into Hassan's eyes, Manny nodded. "Yes."

"Yes, who?"

"Yes, Daddy."

My baby's body was engulfed in pure paternal affection and love. Breaking the embrace, Hassan palmed the back of Manny's head and rested his forehead against Manny's.

"Go finish getting ready for school. I need to talk to your mother."

"Okay!" Manny took off, his feet pounding up the stairs. "Zuri! Kali! Daddy is my daddy, too!"

I wanted to yell up the stairs to tell Manny to quiet it down so he wouldn't wake Chantel. But all I could do was stare back into Hassan's eyes as he gazed at me. Hassan stood, pulled me to him, his hands palming my hips. I wrapped my arms around his waist. My heart pounded in my chest. I was sure Hassan could feel it as our bodies were fused together.

"Ella, you know I love you."

"I do. And I love you, too."

"I don't want to wait to marry you. To give you and Manny my name. To take care of you both like a man is supposed to do for his family."

Woozy, my grip tightened on Hassan's waist to keep from falling. "I don't want to wait either, Hassan. I never believed there was anyone who would come along and love me and my son until you. I want to be your wife and raise our children together in a home full of love and security."

"Then let's do it."

I laid my head on his chest. His heart was beating as fiercely as mine.

"I'm ready. Let's do it."

Twenty-Four

The next two weeks were a blur. Hassan wasted no time making my parents and grandparents aware of his intentions to marry me and legally adopt Manny. I hated to do it, but I had to turn down business in order to have a proper work-life balance. Honestly, I didn't care about the fanfare of planning for our intimate nuptials. I left most of it to Mom and Chantel as I focused on packing mine and Manny's things to move into Hassan's four-bedroom, three-bathroom home. I wasn't ashamed to admit that I cried like a baby when it dawned on me that once Hassan and I married it would be the end of me and my sister living together. Chantel had held me and promised, "I'm not going anywhere. I'm staying right here in this house. I'll even let the kids come stay with me so you and Hassan can have alone time."

The knock on the glass door pulled me out of my reverie. Granddad X and Mom were on the outside waving at me. Excited, I jogged the short distance to open the door. They had Ilona's aka LoLo Rivers' watercolor paintings with them that my grandfather had gifted me to put on display in the gallery. I didn't have to do much convincing for my grandfather to allow me to borrow Ilona's treasure trove of paintings and photographs tucked away in a storage facility to rotate in the gallery. It was important to me that younger generations coming up in Colemanville knew about her and appreciated the beauty of her work.

"Hey, Mom and Granddad X."

We exchanged hugs before they entered. Mom hadn't been by since the renovations were completed. I held my breath as she scrutinized every nook and cranny of the gallery area. She stopped in front of the portrait of Miss Iva Rae I had painted sitting on an easel.

"Oh, Ella...this is beautiful." Tears were in her eyes when she looked at me. The breadth of my mother's love filled every cell in my body. "Grandmother would be proud of you. I'm proud of you."

Granddad X had eased up beside me and rested his hand on my shoulder. "She sure would be."

I patted my grandfather's hand, too choked up to utter a word.

"Show me your studio."

"Right this way."

"I'm gonna stay down here. My knees can't take those stairs today."

"Sit down and rest, Daddy. We won't be long," Mom said as she followed me upstairs to the studio area.

In a far corner was an easel I had covered with a white sheet. Mom gracefully waltzed right on past the ten child sized easels set up in the center of the room, leaving a trail of gardenia perfume. After the grand opening of the gallery, I would be giving art lessons on Mondays and Wednesdays after school to elementary school students. But she didn't inquire about that.

Lifting the sheet, her grin was impish. My mother knew

better. She knew artists were ridiculously secretive about their work until it was ready to be revealed.

"What is under here?"

Playfully, I rolled my eyes. "Mother..."

Mom pouted. "Oh, come on, Ella. Just a little peek."

I wanted to tell her no. How could I? When she was putting in so much effort to mend our splintered relationship.

"Just a peek."

Carefully, she removed the fabric and gazed at the painting for several seconds before looking out the window. Colemanville didn't have an expansive skyline like other cities where I'd lived. Yet, that didn't make it any less magical.

"Will this be for sale?"

I hadn't decided if I wanted to sell this piece or not. Early Saturday mornings before sunrise, while Manny and Chantel were still sleeping, I would drive over to the gallery to paint. That first predawn morning I'd shown up here out of sorts, needing just a moment's reprieve from the chaos in my life trying to consume me. Spirit depressed, my gaze wandered out the window and my eyes were drawn to the church's steeple where my family had belonged since the founding of this town, where my parents had dedicated me and my sister to the Lord as infants. Schools I had attended with childhood friends from elementary to high school. The town square where sightings of Liberty had been seen standing sentinel for generations of the families she had sacrificed her life for so one day they... we would be free. The reflection of the rising sun shimmering off of Copper Lake. A voice I had never heard whispered to me in a tone I could only describe as angelic, "Paint with your heart. That's your strength, Ella."

No one would ever believe me if I told them every time I picked up my brush and watercolor paints, I'd go into a trance-like state. It was almost as if it wasn't me painting. The first time it freaked me out and I swore I wasn't going back to the studio that time of morning again by myself. The following Saturday when three o'clock in the morning rolled around, I found myself getting out of bed, driving to the studio, and in front of my easel, gazing out the window. That time I embraced the trance. With it came a peace that chased away the chaos.

"I haven't decided if I'm going to sell it or not."

"Keeping it for yourself, huh?"

Going over to stand beside my mom, I stared at the painting. Usually, I would find something to criticize about my work. Not this time though. Each time I tried to find something, "paint from your heart" would echo in my mind.

"I think I will keep it."

"Humph, I don't blame you. The sunrise over Colemanville is breathtaking."

A smile curved my lips. As I was blending the orange, red, pink, and yellow colors to recreate the beauty of God's sunrise on canvas that same voice had whispered, "In due time you're going to rise like the sun."

I linked my arm through my mom's and steered us in the direction of the stairs. "Thanks, Mom. You better get Granddad X back home."

"Owen and I are taking Mama and Daddy out to dinner tonight. You and Hassan want to come along?"

"Not this time. We're going shopping with the kids after school to get their clothes for the wedding."

Mom stopped in the middle of the staircase. "Oh, no. I wanted to go with the girls to get their dresses too."

"It's okay, Mom. You've done more than enough."

The ceremony and reception for fifty of our closest friends and family was being held at a swanky wedding venue in Fayetteville. Dad and Mom ran off to Vegas weeks ago to elope. My dad had joked since he and Mom hadn't dished out cash on a lavish second wedding that they would spare no expense for their firstborn's wedding. And they hadn't. The venue, DJ, florist, caterer, and cake designer were the best money could buy. I would have *never* paid what my mother insisted on paying for my wedding dress. I was commanded to hush up when I complained about the expenses she and Dad were footing to pay for my wedding. "Stop fretting over money. Your father and I have been saving for this your entire life."

My mother cut her eyes at me. "Still doesn't stop me from wanting to go with you and my granddaughters."

If we weren't in such a time crunch, I would've pushed back our shopping trip until tomorrow. Hassan taught an evening class at FSU on Thursdays and I wouldn't ask him to miss teaching a class to accommodate my mother. Besides, Mom would insist on us going into a dozen stores and dinner afterwards. It was a school night and Hassan and I had already mapped out our plan. I was taking the girls to the boutique to get their dresses. Hassan would take Manny to Jos. A. Banks to get his suit. Afterwards we would meet up for dinner and head back home so the kids could do their homework and get ready for bed.

"Let's plan a shopping trip for the holidays. I'm sure the girls would like to get a few things for their winter wardrobes."

Mom wrinkled her nose, looking like a Black Samantha Stevens from *Bewitched*. "I guess I'll have to wait until then."

Hassan and my grandfather chuckled at the conversation Mom and I were having coming down the stairs.

"What are you two handsome fellas laughing at?" Mom inquired, beaming at Hassan.

"Nothing at all. How's your day going, Miss Beautiful?"

Mom blushed at Hassan's flirting.

"That's what's wrong with Rosaline..." Granddad X gave his daughter a withering look. "Always could make a man melt right there where he stood with those pretty doe eyes."

"Oh, Daddy, you're exaggerating. That's simply not true."

Me and Hassan cracked up at my mother's embellished southern belle accent.

"It *is* true, Mom."

We all laughed when I recalled how she acted the first time she introduced me and Hassan after church.

"That was for your benefit, dear heart. I had to put my best foot forward when introducing my daughter to Colemanville's most eligible bachelor. Don't you dare deny how all the single ladies at church fawned over you until Ella moved back home. You know those old biddies were orchestrating which one of their daughters or granddaughters was going to marry you."

Now Mom wasn't exaggerating at all about that. Shortly after Hassan and I started dating, Chantel and I were in the supermarket. Moseying down the aisle and minding our business, we heard someone say my name. I hadn't paid much attention to it. The town was abuzz with Colemanville being revitalized. People were talking about the old catering hall being turned into an art gallery and photography studio.

Chantel had put her hand on the shopping cart to halt my movement. She had put her finger to her lips to quiet me. "Listen," she mouthed.

On the other side of the aisle, we heard the voices of three older women gossiping about how I'd come back to town and snatched up Hassan.

"And she has a little boy. My granddaughter doesn't have any children. You would think a handsome man like that wouldn't want a woman with baggage."

"I don't think she's ever been married either... That family always has some scandal or another going on. The old folks say Miss Ilona was still married to her first husband when she started messing around with Gabe Thurman."

Before I could stop Chantel, she whirled around to the other side of the aisle with the force of a tornado. "My nephew is *not* baggage. And keep my great-grandmother's name out of your mouth."

In Chantel fashion, my sister brought *down* the hammer. Didn't give, as my mom called them, the old biddies a chance to brace themselves from the blows.

"In case you haven't figured it out, Miss Vivian, your granddaughter, prefers her girlfriend. Hassan ain't got nothing she wants."

My eyeballs almost popped out of my head. I think Chantel had made that up to give that meddlesome woman angina. I almost felt sorry for the old lady.

To the woman who brought up Ilona, Chantel had locked eyes with her. "Why don't you tell Miss Helen how you've been sleeping with her son since he was in high school?"

Now *that* Chantel hadn't made up. Miss Helen's son, Stephen, was a few years ahead of me in school. It was rumored that he was caught sneaking out of Miss Gladys's back door at the crack of dawn when he was a senior in high school.

All hell had broken loose.

"You molested my child!" Miss Helen slapped Miss Gladys so hard her glasses flew across the aisle. Miss Gladys slapped her back, knocking Miss Helen into stacked cans of tuna. Miss Vivian wasn't having any parts of her friends cutting up in aisle nine. She and her cart scurried off in the opposite direction.

Before my guilt could make me breakup the older women hurling insults and slaps at each other, the store manager had come to the rescue. Chantel and I went about our business finishing our grocery shopping.

As much as I loved the community of a small town, the downside was that sooner or later *everyone* was all up in your business. My grandparents had shared Ilona and Gabe's love story with all of us grandchildren. Their reasoning had been to squash the gossip fest Chantel and I had stumbled upon.

"Am I telling the truth or not, Hassan?"

Hassan let out an exasperated breath. "Thought I was the last turkey and it was Thanksgiving morning."

"You were the last turkey," Granddad X cracked.

Mom and I laughed. She gave me a pointed look. "Don't you think for one minute those women still aren't scheming."

"They can scheme all they want." Hassan pulled me to him. I wrapped my arms around his waist. "My heart is right here."

I appreciated my mom's warning. But I was far past the age of getting into a cat fight over a man. Besides, I wasn't worried about Hassan's affections straying elsewhere.

"Same here." I kissed Hassan's cheek.

Approvingly, my grandfather smiled at us. "Put God first in your relationship and you'll be alright."

Mom touched Granddad X's arm. "You ready, Daddy?"

"I'm ready. Before we go, Ella, come see where I hung the paintings."

We all went over to the area of the gallery dedicated to Ilona's work. Chantel and I had already hung five pieces of her work we had in our collection. I'd left three blank spaces to hang *Graceful Watercolors* and *The Marriage Bed*. The other space would include the plaque Chantel was working on that would highlight Ilona's history as an artist.

"Thanks, Granddad X. This is perfect."

We hugged and said our goodbyes to my mom and grandfather. Once they were gone, Hassan pulled me in for a kiss that made me want to speed up our marriage date. Two weeks might as well have been next year.

"Let's elope like Mom and Dad," I moaned, pressing into Hassan's hard body.

"Don't tempt me, woman."

"Mom would never forgive me."

Hassan chuckled. "Nope. I'm on her good side. Don't want to mess that up."

As I was about to say, "Let's get out of here," my phone buzzed in my back pocket. I glanced at the display.

"It's Silas. Should I answer?"

The kids were excited for our mid-week shopping trip and the promise of going out to eat afterwards. I didn't want us to be late picking them up.

"Yeah, could be important."

"Hey, Silas. What's going on?"

My upbeat mood took a dive from the tone of Silas's voice.

"Alright...okay...yes, I understand."

I pressed the heel of my hand into my forehead. Every time my life felt like some semblance of peace was on the horizon, Preston's evil aura tainted it.

"What's wrong, babe?"

"Silas wants me to come to his office."

"Now?"

"Yes."

"Let's go."

Twenty-Five

Vision blurred, I stared into Hassan's eyes as he recited his vows to me.

"Ella, I promise to love you unconditionally. To be your strength and your protector. I will always value you as my equal. I will love Emanuel as my son with my entire heart. Before God, I promise you our circle will never be broken."

When it came my turn to say the vows I had written, my voice, although trembling, was strong and resolute.

"Hassan, I never dreamed of loving a man like you. Not because I didn't want to. I simply didn't believe you existed. Now that I know you are as real as the sun, moon, and stars, I will not only love you with every breath that I take, I will always honor and respect you." I turned to face Zuri and Kali. "From this moment and forever, your beautiful girls belong to me."

The girls grabbed each other's hands and mouthed, "We love you, Mom."

Our family and friends released a collective, dreamy sigh when I affirmed my love to Zuri and Kali. "I love you too, my precious babies."

At last, we came to the part where the pastor announced, "You may now salute your bride."

Every dream and hope of being loved and cherished was perfected in Hassan's kiss. If it hadn't been for Grandma Rose yelling out, "Young man, let my grandbaby up for some air," we would still be kissing.

Fingers threaded, Hassan and I made our way around to greet our guests during the cocktail hour. Jillian and I hugged each other tightly. Hassan and her husband Ivan greeted each other in a handshake, exchanging pleasantries.

"I'm so happy for you, Ella."

"Thank you for being here, Jillian."

"Girl, where else would I be?"

Her words made me hug her even tighter. In my immaturity, I hadn't been there to celebrate Jillian's or Kristen's weddings. Too stubborn and in my feelings about them betraying our childhood pact, I chose not to be a friend. Something I would always regret.

"I wish Kristen could've made it."

Humbling myself, weeks ago I reached out to Jillian for Kristen's number since they'd remained in touch throughout the years. Our conversation had been pleasant enough, though awkward. I told her I was sorry to hear about her husband's death from Jillian. I thought it was strange that she immediately jumped to asking me about moving back to Colemanville. It was as if she didn't want my condolences. When I called again to invite her to my wedding, she had said she couldn't make it on such short notice and apologized.

"Me too. I'm trying to talk her into coming down for the Christmas holiday."

"I would love that. I hope she will consider doing so."

"Come on, babe, let's greet the rest of our guests."

I gave Jillian another squeeze before we made our way over to my new in-laws. Hassan's parents, Rhoda and Milton, and his brothers Kofi and Amari. His mother engulfed me in an embrace that bordered on smothering. I welcomed every bit of it. I was a bit apprehensive to meet Hassan's family when they arrived in town a few days ago. His father and brothers were accepting. Miss Rhoda's reception was a bit frosty. So much so even the girls had noticed. Zuri had followed me into the kitchen where I went back to preparing lunch for them. "My grandmom is a nice lady. She just didn't like how my mom treated my dad."

I wanted to scream, "I'm not your mother."

Later that evening I invited Miss Rhoda out to brunch the following day. We had an open and honest conversation that lasted three hours. By the time we left the restaurant, she had given me her blessing to marry her eldest child.

"I *finally* have a daughter. I know you're gonna treat my son right."

"Yes, you do. And I'm gonna love him like he's never been loved." I leaned back from the embrace, my arms still wrapped around her back. "What should I call you?"

"Girl! I just called you my daughter and you're asking what you should call me?"

"Mama," Hassan groaned. His dad and brothers chuckled.

"Ma'am, I'm so sorry. Mama it is."

My bonus mother grinned bashfully when I kissed her on the cheek. I was looking forward to getting to know my new family. After hugging my father-in-law and brothers-in-law, Hassan and I continued to greet and talk with guests until the waitstaff was ready to serve dinner.

During dinner our family members went to the mic and told embarrassing stories about the both of us growing up. Nana Flo went to the mic first.

"Now, I ain't blood, but I am family. Ella's great-grandmother, Ilona, was my mother's friend. She and the rest of the DOLLs looked after me after my mama passed away. I promised Ilona I would look after her grandbabies *and* great-grandbabies the same way she looked after me."

Nana Flo pointed her cane at me. "And that's what I did. Tore Ella, Jillian, and Kristen's hind parts up with my switch when I caught them behind the barn smoking them funny cigarettes when they were in high school. Back there giggling like a bunch of hyenas."

The entire room was cracking up. Mortified at my own wedding, I buried my face in Hassan's chest to hide my flushing.

Nana Flo wasn't finished though. She held her hand up to silence everyone. "Baby, Ilona and Gabe are smiling down on you and Hassan. May your love story be as wonderful and last as long as theirs did."

I blew kisses at Nana Flo as Jillian's husband escorted her back to their table.

After the last guest said their well wishes, the DJ cranked up the music. In addition to the traditional wedding dances, Manny and I danced together, as did Hassan and our girls. While holding Manny close to me, I said a prayer, thanking God that the nightmare with Preston was finally over. That day when Silas called me at the gallery to come to his office, Hassan and I rushed over, not knowing what to expect. All Silas would say during that short conversation was that there was a new development concerning Preston.

When we arrived, Silas was waiting for us in the lobby and ushered us inside his office, telling his administrative assistant to hold his calls.

Once the door was closed, he motioned for us to have a seat. I'd never forget the foreboding feeling I had in my gut. I had expected Silas to tell us that Preston was on the run. Hassan had taken my hand and held it tightly.

"Another woman has surfaced."

Annoyed, I had rolled my eyes and was ready to get up and

leave. We had things to do and I wasn't interested in hearing about Preston's debauchery into a black hole of horrible behavior. My hand was on my purse and I was about to stand.

"The woman was seventeen at the time." That stopped me in my tracks and I flopped back down on the sofa. This whole ordeal was trying to suck the life out of me.

"Apparently, Preston had been friends with her parents. The young lady did admit that she was the one who made advances toward Preston. Their fling lasted until she was twenty and went to study abroad. The relationship ended when she met and fell in love with a classmate."

"Why is she coming forward if she made the advances? I mean, jackass should've known better and rebuffed her."

Hassan had grunted in disgust. "He's a damn predator, Ella. In his sick mind he didn't see anything wrong with it."

"Well, it backfired on him. She wasn't the one to come forward. It was her parents. The mother had overheard a conversation between their daughter and Preston years ago. When confronted they both admitted the affair, but swore it was over. At the time the daughter was twenty-five and engaged to a foreign diplomat and Preston was dating..." Silas waved his hand in the air. "Some actress. Apparently, the parents didn't want any negative press surfacing and tainting their daughter's nuptials."

"Who is the woman? And why did we have to rush over here?" I had asked, irritated.

Silas words had come out of his mouth in slow motion. "Rachel...Adler."

"Oh, damn," Hassan had murmured.

The Adler family was old money from Georgia that made their wealth in the pharmaceutical industry dating back to the late eighteen hundreds. The family prided themselves on philanthropic causes supporting the arts. According to Silas, the couple had befriended Preston and felt betrayed when he crossed the line and slept with their underage daughter. Their motive for coming forward now was revenge.

"Preston's housekeeper found him in his car in the garage with the engine running and the windows up. By the time they got him to the hospital, it was too late. District Attorney Abrams called me right away. She didn't want you to find out about it on the news."

Stunned, I sat there speechless for ten minutes. I wouldn't wish death on anyone, not even Preston. However, I did want him to be held accountable for trying to kidnap Manny and what he had done to me and the other women. Taking his own life was the coward's way out. Part of me was relieved that I wouldn't have to go to court and dredge up painful memories. And that Manny wouldn't have to be afraid that someday Preston would attempt to kidnap him again.

On the ride home Hassan and I had discussed how we would tell Manny about Preston's death. Later that evening we sat down with our son. He had looked from me to Hassan. "That man won't bother us anymore?"

When I answered, "No, baby." Manny had pumped his fist. "Yes! He wasn't a nice man, Mommy."

As wicked as Preston was, I never wished death on him. Yet part of me did rejoice in knowing that my child wouldn't have to live under the shadow of fear. Hassan and I had already determined when Manny was old enough, we would tell him everything. We didn't want there to be any lurking secrets. Besides, no matter how well one might think a secret was buried, it always clawed its way to the surface. Especially nowadays with social media, blogs, and podcasts. Until that time came, our mission was to love on our son and raise him the best we knew how with the support of our families.

"Mommy wants you to be good while me and Daddy are gone for a few days."

For our wedding gift, my grandparents paid for our honeymoon for a four-night, all-inclusive, private villa in Belize. Although I was looking forward to uninterrupted time with my husband, I had a bit of apprehension about leaving the children.

"I'm gonna be good for Auntie Chantel. Can Noah spend the night?"

I glanced across the dance floor and smiled at Noah dancing with his mother. Our flight didn't leave until tomorrow afternoon. Hassan had booked the honeymoon suite at a five-star hotel for our wedding night. It had been a long day and I didn't want to ask Chantel to be responsible for looking after another child.

"Not tonight, Manny. When me and Daddy get back home we'll pick a Friday or Saturday night for Noah to come over."

Sullen, Manny mumbled, "Okay."

I stooped down so I was eye level with him. "Remember the talk we had about you not always getting your way?"

Manny nodded.

"Well, this is one of those times. I'm sure you and Noah will see each other tomorrow. Now stop all that pouting. Give me a smile."

The photographer eased up to us and snapped a picture.

I hugged Manny and sent him off to go be with his friend. My next stop was to the table where our families were seated. A sigh escaped my lips as I flopped down beside my dad. He put his arm around my shoulder and kissed my temple. "Baby doll, you're a beautiful bride." He winked at my mother. "Almost as beautiful as your mother on our wedding day."

Grandma Rose, still feeling some kind of way about my parents eloping, drawled, "Which wedding day?"

Granddad X and I shared a look. I gazed across the room at Chantel and Silas swaying together to an old school Babyface love ballad to keep from laughing. My grandfather was weary of his beloved beating a dead horse concerning my parents' elopement.

"Oh, Mama. How many times do I have to apologize?" Mom snapped politely, clearly bothered by the comment which got her a stern glare from my grandmother.

"Until I get tired of hearing it! Y'all sneaking around like you're teenagers!" Grandma Rose snapped back. Clearly unbothered by the fact that she was at her granddaughter's wedding airing her grievances.

"Rose, leave my daughter alone. She and Owen ain't did no harm. I'm pleased they're back together." Granddad X raised a gray bushy brow at my father. "I was *tired* of seeing Owen's car parked around the corner from Rosaline's house every night."

Mom's face turned three shades of red. Dad chuckled, causing me to playfully elbow him in the side.

I had to come to Mom's defense. "Leave my mother alone. We all knew someday they'd get back together again."

After my parents' divorce, things weren't weird between them. Chantel and I never felt like we had to take sides as kids or choose between our parents. Mom and Dad could create a manual on how to effectively co-parent.

Through the years, at different family events, I would notice my dad giving Mom lingering stares. And Mom pretending not to be affected by Dad's admiration of her. I didn't have the nerve to ask Mom how long her and Dad had been *sneaking* around. So I went to Dad. A feather could've knocked me over when he confessed the timing of their rekindled romance. Talk about creeping. My folks started casually seeing each other again off and on not long after I had given birth to Manny. Three years ago, they recommitted to being together.

"I'm happy Mom and Dad are back together." I raised my

glass. "To Mom and Dad. May divorce never be in your future again."

In the middle of toasting the second time around newlyweds, Hassan sauntered over to the table. He leaned down and whispered in my ear. "I'm ready to go."

My insides quivered at his smoldering gaze. We'd already had our first dance and cut the cake. At our ages, we decided to forgo the bouquet and garter tossing. There was nothing holding us back from leaving. I placed the glass on the table.

"So am I."

Twenty-Six

The second the elevator doors closed, Hassan pulled me to him and backed me against the mirrored wall. Our bodies fused intimately. The evidence of his desire pressed against me caused me to lean in harder so I could feel more of him. When our mouths met in a feverish kiss, I felt out of control. Free. Uninhibited.

I'd dreamt about what it would be like to make love to Hassan. There were times we'd both had to chase the other home otherwise we'd end up consummating the relationship and risking one of our children stumbling on something their innocent eyes had no business bearing witness to. We wanted to set examples for our children. It had bothered Hassan that the girls' mother had moved them in with her boyfriend, exposing them to a lifestyle of shacking up. I respected him even more that he wouldn't be a hypocrite and lived by his own morals.

When the soft chime sounded, signaling we had arrived at the twenty-sixth floor, Hassan threaded his fingers through mine. I couldn't help giggling. He was practically dragging me with his long strides down the corridor. As he stood in front of me, fumbling with the keycard, I wrapped my arms around his waist and laid my cheek against his wide back. Inhaling the scent of his cologne was a drug. I was woozy. High on love. He allowed me to stay that way for several seconds before he glanced over his shoulder at me.

"Ella?"

The concern in his voice for me made me want to cry. It was all still so surreal. The shattered pieces of my life had fallen into place in the most unexpected, beautifully amazing way.

"I'm good, Hassan. Just soaking up reality. This is real. *You're real*. I'm real."

Turning, his calloused hands framed my face. "I love you, Ella Murphy."

"And I love you, Hassan Murphy."

Hassan swept me up in his arms and carried me to the king sized bed. He sat on the side of the bed with me on his lap. My head fell back as he kissed my neck and along my collarbone. His hand slowly and expertly unzipped my dress, sending wanton chills down my spine. Taking his time, Hassan removed our clothing until we were both as the day we were born. My hand trembled as my fingertips touched his bare chest and traveled down the solid muscles of his abdomen until I was holding him in my hand.

We gazed into each other's eyes as my hand tenderly stroked his hardness. A mixture of pleasure and torture contorted his handsome features. Hassan's tight, yet gentle grasp on my wrist held me captive. I didn't resist when he laid me on the bed and kissed me for what seemed like an eternity, leaving me wanting my husband like I'd never wanted another man. There was no use in rushing him along. Long before this night came, I knew Hassan would be the kind of lover that would savor every touch, every kiss. And he did not disappoint.

Twenty-six stories up there was no need to close the ceiling to floor drapes. The moonlight streaming through the large window illuminated Hassan's dark skin. I couldn't take my gaze off of him as he kissed between the valley of my breasts. My eyes fluttered shut as he lavished attention on my breasts before planting kiss after kiss down my body until he feasted on me. I didn't try to harness the screams erupting from me as I exploded in pure ecstasy.

When my husband joined our bodies as one, there was no singular word my brain could formulate to describe the emotions I was experiencing. Love. Trust. Euphoria. Satisfaction. Too many to name.

Hands above our heads, fingers laced, my legs wrapped around his waist, we locked gazes. A tear slid out the corner of my eye. I saw nothing but devotion in good and bad times. Us being loving parents to our three children. Another tear escaped as my heart dreamt of the possibility of Hassan and I creating a life that would further unite us.

Hassan tenderly kissed the tracks of my tears. "Baby, I'll give you whatever you want."

Were we that in sync that he could decipher my innermost longings? God, I hoped so.

Before I could utter my heart's desire, my body trembled again in sweet release. Hassan followed me. Untangling our fingers, he held me in a snug embrace. My arms wrapped around his neck. I could feel his heart pounding against my chest. We stayed that way, interlinked as one form. I closed my eyes, padlocking every detail in the vaults of my heart and mind to recapture this moment later on canvas.

When my husband's weight became too heavy for me to bear, I shifted my body beneath his. He rolled over onto his back. Curling into his side, my head on his chest, the sound of his beating heart soothed me like a lullaby.

"Did you mean what you just said?"

His rich chuckle turned my insides to mush.

"Ella, baby...I've said a lot to you."

Laughing, I playfully slapped his chest. "Don't be like that, Hassan."

He grabbed my hand and placed a lingering kiss on my wrist. "Of course, I did." He lifted my chin so we were looking at each other.

"Ella, I'll never withhold anything from you."

"Not even a baby?"

His grin matched the brightness of the moonlight shining through the night sky.

"Aww, damn. Girl, you're speaking my love language."

Leaning up on my elbow, I ran my fingers through his locs, loving the feel of the texture between my fingers. It felt like soft cotton. "We'll start trying in six months to a year?"

In anticipation of a healthy sex life, I'd scheduled an appointment with my GYN and had an IUD inserted. Neither of us had broached the baby conversation. I supposed because we already had three active children we were raising.

Hassan nuzzled his nose against my neck. "We can start trying now?"

I straddled my husband and ran my hands up his chest. A coy smile curved my lips. "We can practice for now."

OUR FOUR-DAY HONEYMOON was entirely too brief, yet every moment was well cherished. I couldn't remember the last time I'd laid in bed until after ten in the morning. I would wake to find Hassan sitting outside our villa in Belize staring at the ocean. We'd order breakfast and, after showering, take long walks on the beach, holding hands and dreaming about our future. After dinner we'd go to the nightclub on the island and dance until we were sticky and sweaty. I'd forgotten how much I used to enjoy dancing. It didn't hurt that Hassan had moves. Being exhausted didn't stop us from making love until the dawn of a new day. Chantel and

Silas frequently went out to a nightclub in Jacksonville that catered to an over thirty-five crowd. On the plane ride home, we promised to go out dancing once a month with Chantel and Silas.

We were tempted to stay a few days longer. Those days Hassan and I spent in a world where only we existed were glorious. No coordinating schedules to pick kids up from after school activities, rushing home to prepare meals, or helping with school projects interfered. We weren't ashamed to admit we wanted to languish a bit longer in seclusion. But each time we called home to check on the kids, Manny wanted to know when we were coming home. "I miss you and Daddy."

At his age he didn't have a concept of time. I was sure our being away felt like weeks to him instead of days.

On the front porch, Hassan looked over his shoulder at me. "You sure you don't want to hop a plane back to Belize?"

I didn't think I'd ever get bored with that sexy grin he was giving me.

"No. I'm not sure. Especially with you looking at me like that."

His kiss was sweet.

"You complaining?" he mumbled against my lips.

"Not at all."

When Hassan opened the door to what was now me and Manny's new home, Manny was on his knees at the coffee table. Matchbox cars were scattered over the surface of the furniture. He had a car in each hand that he forcefully pushed along the length of the table in a race. Engrossed in his playing, he hadn't noticed us entering.

It wasn't until Hassan dropped the duffle bag loaded with gifts for the kids and Chantal at the front door, causing a soft thump, that Manny's head popped up.

"Mommy! Daddy!"

I kneeled to welcome my baby boy leaping into my arms.

"Hey, baby."

Manny clinging to me made tears spring to my eyes. I loved this little boy more than my own life.

"You and Daddy was gone forever."

Hassan ruffled the curls on Manny's head. "We're back now."

The girls, along with Chantel on their heels, emerged from the kitchen. Zuri and Kali were just as excited to see us. They ran to Hassan for hugs, then to me.

"Move out the way and let me get to my sister and brother."

We all laughed at Chantel swinging her hips from side to side as if knocking over objects in her way.

She grabbed me in a tight embrace. "Girl, I love my nieces and nephew. But next time y'all gonna have to take us. I'll babysit the entire time."

Chantel released me to hug Hassan.

"What happened?"

Zuri giggled. "Manny and Kali kept asking Auntie Chantel when you and Dad were coming home. They kept asking to call y'all."

Pretending offense, Chantel patted her hand on the center of her chest. "Like I'm not the best auntie ever."

"You are," Kali promised. She eased up beside me and wrapped her arms around my waist. "We just missed you both, Mommy."

I kissed her forehead. "Aww, baby, we missed y'all too." I grinned at my daughter. "But me and your dad deserved our honeymoon."

"We know. Did y'all have fun? I know you took a lot of pictures," Zuri rushed out. Out of the two girls, Zuri was taking a liking to photography. I didn't know that until Granddad X showed the children a camera that Gabe had given Ilona for her thirtieth birthday one afternoon. Zuri was intrigued with the vintage equipment.

"I did. We can look through them together later." I'd let her help me pick out photos to make postcards to send to our wedding guests as thank you notes.

Hassan picked up our luggage and headed toward the stairs. "Let me and your mother take our luggage upstairs. We'll be back down in a few minutes."

"Okay, please hurry. Me and Kali were helping Auntie Chantel make a taco bar for lunch."

"Oh, that sounds yummy. We'll be right back."

I followed Hassan up the stairs to what once was his bedroom. While we were gone Chantel had asked if she could freshen up the space. The dark furnishings and black and gray tones gave off a masculine vibe. Hassan gave his blessing to make our sleeping and lounging quarters an area where I would be comfortable too. I had made my sister promise to make sure Hassan would enjoy the space as well. "Don't get carried away, Chantel."

The door was closed with a hand painted sign in a fancy font that read: Welcome Home, Newlyweds. Slowly, I turned the door knob. Open windows allowed the white drapes to billow carelessly. The flatscreen television mounted on the wall freed up space on the dresser to display my perfumes on a mirrored tray. Hassan's colognes were arranged on a black leather tray. On the king sized bed was a hotel quality white duvet and pillows. A plush gray throw was draped across the foot of the bed. Over the bed hung the painting of Colemanville at sunrise my mother had wanted to purchase from me. The black chaise lounge that was in my bedroom sat in a corner. Chantel had replaced the bold colored decorative pillows I had on the chaise to colors that complemented the hues in the painting.

The way Hassan's gaze moved around the room, I could tell he was impressed.

"Wow, this looks like a different room. I see Chantel hung your painting. It's beautiful."

Tilting my head, I stared at my work. Each day I woke up I was going to enjoy visualizing the vibrant colors of a gorgeous sunrise no matter the weather outside.

"Thank you. Our bedroom was the perfect place for it." I gazed at my husband. "If I hadn't come back to Colemanville, I wouldn't be standing here...right now...with you."

Hassan eased up behind me and wrapped his arms around my waist. I leaned into him for support, figuratively and literally. I believed him when he told me, "This is where you belong."

Before I could turn in his arms to kiss him, someone was knocking on the door. Ignoring the knocking, I kissed him. He backed me toward the bed. Whichever kid was on the other side of the door was persistent with the knocking.

He groaned when I whispered against his lips, "Welcome home."

Twenty-Seven

Grand Opening of Art Gallery
Second Friday of November

"Wow, look at all those people," Kali gushed as we pulled up in our seven seater SUV.

"My friend Yolanda from school said she and her parents were coming," Zuri chimed in.

I wanted to revel in my daughters' enthusiasm, but my nerves were stretched like a rubber band past its resistance. A majority of the invitees had RSVPed to the opening. That didn't stop me from having a restless night, tossing and turning, worried if folks were actually going to show up. To calm me, Hassan had rolled over and draped his arm over my midsection. With a tender kiss to the nape of my neck, he whispered, "Baby, get some sleep and stop stressing."

Lying in his arms had temporarily calmed me. As the day went on, everything that could go wrong went wrong. The girls' mother called Hassan complaining that *her* daughters hadn't been calling her weekly as they should. When Hassan kindly informed her, "You're their mother, what's wrong with you reaching out to them too?" all hell broke loose. His ex sounded like a squawking bird on the other end of the phone, cussing Hassan out from here to next Tuesday. Instead of arguing, he hung up on her.

Of all days, Manny and Noah decided *today* was a good day to climb a tree. Manny ended up tumbling to the ground on his way down when I called the boys in for a snack. Scared out of my mind seeing my baby laying on the ground in the backyard, I dashed out the back door. Every time I touched the arm he landed on, Manny howled in pain. I ended up having to take him to the emergency room to get checked out. Thank goodness it was a sprain and not a broken bone. Although Noah's mother had planned on attending the opening, she offered to stay home with the boys.

Now that my fear of not having a decent turnout had been for nothing, that dread was replaced with second guessing my work. Would people like it? Did I select the right pieces to show? How would they react to Ilona's work?

I glanced over my shoulder at the girls. The look of pure admiration on their faces squashed the imposter syndrome threatening to make me hyperventilate and break out in hives. My family loved and supported me. My community supported me. I was going to roll with that and have a great time. And be thankful for every individual who came out to celebrate the opening of my art gallery. Hopefully, I would sell a few paintings or photographs.

"I was anxious people weren't going to show up." Glancing over at Hassan, I smiled. "I kept your dad up tossing and turning last night. Zuri, be sure to introduce me to Yolanda and her parents."

"Okay, I will."

Hassan pulled into the spot that had been blocked off for

us to park. Chantel had done a fabulous job painting The Ella Collective: Art and Photography in a sleek, modern font in gold across the center glass window.

He got out of the vehicle and helped me out before helping Zuri and Kali out. My heart was pounding as I entered the gallery on my husband's arm. Folks were milling around, nibbling on hors d'oeuvres. Some were in small groups gathered around paintings or photographs. Others were sipping on champagne and talking.

Someone recognized me and called out, "There's Ella."

I didn't expect the thunderous clapping and cheering. We were greeted by hugs from folks in the community. My family was gathered in the area where I had displayed Ilona aka LoLo Rivers' work. Grandma Rose excitedly waved us over.

"Excuse me, Mayor Riley. You know I can't keep Grandma Rose waiting."

She chuckled. "No, you can't keep Miss Rose waiting. Before you go, I'd like to set up an appointment with you in a few weeks to discuss hosting an event in the new year."

Digging in my clutch, I handed Mayor Riley a business card to contact me.

Grandma Rose gave me a big squeeze. Framing my face in her hands, tears were in her eyes. "Baby, I'm so proud of you. I know Mama Ilona and Daddy Gabe are smiling down on you."

"Stop, Grandma Rose. You're going to make me cry."

"You always were a crybaby, Ella Caswell."

I swung around so fast, I almost fell. Jillian and my friend since toddlerhood were standing beside each other. I didn't care if my shouting was considered unruly.

"Kristen! You're here!"

We locked in a tight embrace, rocking from side to side. I sure hoped the waterproof mascara I had on did what it claimed.

"Girl, I missed you. I'm sorry," I whispered in her ear.

Kristen squeezed me extra tight and I knew we were going to sit down and make things good between us again.

"I missed you too. You're not the only one to have something to be sorry about."

Kristen released me and we held hands, smiling at each other. I held out a hand for Jillian to join us. If no one purchased a painting, I wouldn't care. It couldn't compare to how my heart overflowed being united with my best friends. The circle was once again unbroken.

"Thanks for coming, Kristen."

Out of the three of us, Kristen was the sassy one. Hand on her hip, she raised an eyebrow at me. "Where else would I be? Since we were sixteen you talked about having your own studio or gallery."

"And look at you. You have a studio *and* gallery," Jillian pointed out, playfully poking me in the arm.

"What about you, Miss Jillian?"

Jillian blushed. "Tonight isn't about me. It's about you, Ella."

Kristen rolled her eyes. "Jillian still can't take a compliment. Ugh, Philly girl."

"That's right. Proud of it too," Jillian sassed.

"Leave our friend alone. I want to know what's going on with you, Miss Kristen."

Impish as ever, Kristen smirked, "I want you to introduce me to that handsome husband of yours first."

"Oh, boy," Jillian mumbled, causing us to laugh.

Turning serious, Kristen promised, "Before I leave, I want to have lunch or dinner with you both...to catch you up on the madness that's been my life for the last several years."

Trouble sure didn't have any favorites.

I waved over Hassan and introduced him to Kristen. The two hugged like long lost friends.

"Why do you look so familiar, Hassan?"

Jillian and I snickered.

"What?" Kristen looked from me to Jillian.

"Do you remember Mr. Harvey?"

Kristen grinned and it lit up her face. "Sure do. Remember we took his pretty red Mustang from his auto shop when he and Mrs. Harvey went on vacation." She looked over her shoulder at Nana Flo and my grandparents chatting. "I also remember staying in jail all night and getting a tail whipping from Nana Flo the next day."

Cracking up, I looped my arm through Hassan's and leaned into his side. "My hubby is Mr. Harvey's nephew."

"Wow, what a small world. I wonder what happened to that car? I used to love seeing Mr. and Mrs. Harvey riding around town."

"My uncle left it to me."

Drunk on love, I tilted my head and gazed into my husband's eyes. "The first time I saw Hassan he was driving the Mustang."

I'd missed Kristen's wild antics. I almost hooted when she cracked, "Girl, I'mma need you to do some strange things to get them keys to that car! We about to go joy riding. Beep beep!"

Poor Hassan was speechless. I'd never seen his cheeks flush with color before.

We were laughing when Mom came over. She gave her rounds of kisses and hugs. She and Kristen's hug was extra-long. My parents loved Kristen. We were practically raised in each other's homes.

"Ella, I need to steal you for a few minutes."

"Okay, Mom." I blew kisses promising, "I'll catch up with y'all later."

Mom led me over to the other side of the gallery where I

had a set of three eighteen by twenty photographs of the Grand Canyon at sunrise, sunset, and midnight.

"Ella, this is Dr. Johnston and his wife Tabitha. They're interested in purchasing the entire set of photos. Isn't that wonderful?" Mom beamed.

The middle aged couple were art enthusiasts, which I appreciated. I stood there with them answering questions about the photos. The wife, a petite woman with piercing hazel eyes, inquired, "What's the story behind the photographs?

Indeed, there was a story behind the photos. I gave them the watered-down version. Sharing just enough to intrigue them.

That night I went out to capture nature's beauty. My soul was sick, depressed. I was still trying to wrap my head around how in minutes my life was stolen from me. How shame and embarrassment had me caught up in a tangled web of chaos. Terrified my secret would be revealed. Too afraid to stand up to Preston for fear of having my family's legacy tarnished. Or worse, him wanting to stake a claim in Manny's life. After I was done taking at least a hundred shots, I stood on the edge of a cliff. Before leaving the hotel that night, I had contemplated taking my life. Tucked inside a pocket in Manny's diaper bag was a letter I had written begging my family to forgive me and asking Chantel to raise Manny.

I had closed my eyes and before I could step into nothingness, my breasts began to leak. Manny's beautiful face flashed before me and I couldn't do it. It felt as if some invisible force had pushed me back.

When I had gotten back to the hotel room, Chantel was about ready to pull her hair out. Manny had been crying incessantly. Nothing she did soothed him. The second I took him into my arms and he latched onto my breast, he calmed down and drifted off to sleep. I kissed his forehead and promised him no matter how bad things got, I would never let the thought to end my life cross my mind again.

After talking to the couple, I worked the room, greeting my other guests, answering questions about the inspiration for work. The portrait of Miss Iva Rae was on an easel covered in a corner. Moving around the room, I heard whispers wondering what was mysteriously hidden beneath the easel.

The event planner my sister hired to coordinate the opening informed me it was time for me to say a few words and uncover the painting. Nervous jitters caused my legs to shake as she guided me over to the easel before getting everyone's attention.

As I looked out into the faces of the folks who came out to support, many of them I knew. Like Dante Henry and his sister Celeste who, generations later, still owned and operated the lumber mill in rural Colemanville. Former colleagues from the college where I worked and NBA photographers I'd met early in my career were in attendance. Other faces weren't familiar.

Though I loved my husband, who was nearby encouraging me with his prideful smile, I called on my security blanket to stand by my side.

"Chantel, come over here with me."

She hesitated for a moment. Knowing my sister as I did, she wanted this to be all about me. But it wasn't. Throughout my life I had her support along the way to get me to this monumental occasion. This was her rightful place.

Beside me, I grabbed my sister's hand.

"I'm grateful for everyone who has believed in me, supported me." I gazed at my mother on the brink of tears. She turned out to be my biggest cheerleader. "My parents, grandparents...my loving husband...my children. All the neighbors who stopped by during renovations of the gallery to wish me well. Former colleagues and those of you I've never met...thank you for being here tonight."

I touched the crystal hummingbird brooch on the burnt orange dress I was wearing. A gift my great-grandfather Gabe had given his beloved Ilona. Granddad X and Grandma Rose said they both would want me to wear it tonight.

Tears formed in my eyes as I looked toward heaven. "I thank God for bestowing Ilona, my great-grandmother's, gift on me. There are no words to express how this gift has enriched my life. Since I was a teenager, I've dreamed of owning a gallery and studio. For years, I've run from my destiny...instead of toward it."

Chantel squeezed my hand as she wiped at the tears leaking out of the corner of her eyes.

"The one constant I've always had in my life was my sister. When I would lose hope or doubt that this day would come... *my* sister was *always* telling me, 'Ella, you can do this. You got this.' She believed when I didn't. I asked you to be by my side Chantel because I could not have done any of this without you."

Chantel was outright bawling. When we hugged, it felt like time stood still. We stayed that way until the applause died down. Mom handed us both tissues to dry our tears. Someone yelled out, "Gone on and cry. It's alright."

"Now that that's out of the way. I know you're all wondering what's underneath here." I glanced over at Jillian. "We all know that Colemanville has birthed some amazing women. We have our town matriarch with us tonight. Nana Flo, please join me."

Jillian mouthed to me, "What is going on?" as Nana Flo made her way beside me.

I pretended like I didn't see her.

"It's no secret that Jillian gives the best facial this side of North Carolina. We're all anticipating the opening of her day spa in several months. Nana Flo and I conspired to add something special to Jillian's spa." I winked at my accomplice. "You ready, Nana Flo?"

"I sure am, baby."

Chantel assisted Nana Flo to one side of the easel while I stood on the other side. Together, we lifted the covering to reveal the portrait of Iva Rae.

There were a few gasps, followed by applause. Guests moved in closer to get a better look at the painting.

"Beautiful..."

"It's so life-like..."

"Miss Iva Rae was a gorgeous lady..."

Were a few of the comments I overheard before Jillian grabbed and hugged me. "Thank you so much, Ella. I love it."

"You're welcome. I knew you always loved the painting Nana Flo kept of her mother in the shop."

"Yes, but I knew Nana Flo wouldn't hear of parting with her mama's portrait."

"Now she doesn't have to."

Hassan and Ivan approached as we were talking.

"Babe, I'm so proud of you." Hassan beamed, placing a chaste kiss on my lips.

I didn't care if we were in public. I wrapped my arms around my husband's neck and kissed him again. "Thank you."

A photographer from *The Colemanville Chronicle* came over and asked if he could take a picture with me in front of the photo I had enlarged with me as a toddler on Ilona's lap painting.

"I'll be right back," I told Hassan, kissing him again.

Several times, I stopped to thank people for coming as the photographer and I went to the area of the gallery where Ilona's work was displayed.

The photographer got into position to get the shot and

abruptly held his camera down. He tilted his head and stared at me, then the painting to my left. "Your great-grandmother painted that?"

I glanced over my shoulder to gaze at *Graceful Watercolors*. My smile came from the depths of my soul. "Yes, she did."

"What year?"

"Nineteen forty-nine."

"That's amazing. The woman in the painting looks exactly like you."

Granddad X's words came back to me about Ilona painting her visions. I'd like to think Ilona envisioned peace for me that only God's grace could bring.

"It is me."

GENERATIONS: THE SERIES

Book 1: *Forever Beautiful*

Book 2: *Wandering Beauty*

Book 3: *Watercolor Whispers*

Book 4: *Graceful Watercolors*

Book 5: Coming February 2025

Book 6: Coming February 2025

Book 7: Coming May 2025

Book 8: Coming May 2025

Book 9: Coming August 2025

Book 10: Coming August 2025

Book 3

Enjoyed Book 4? Don't stop there! Meet Ella's beautiful ancestor, Ilona Robertson.

Watercolor Whispers
by Suzette D. Harrison

Ilona Robertson Brinks is a gifted artist trapped in a gilded cage. Bound by a controlling husband and stifled by domineering parents, Ilona's world is a portrait of conformity and quiet constraint. Her life is a delicate balance of duty, family expectations, and unspoken dreams. Her art is her great escape from her less than fulfilling reality. Every brushstroke is a private rebellion as the vibrant colors on her canvas whispers the truths she cannot speak. Even more so when confronted with the return of her first love, Gabriel Thurman.

A veteran injured in the war, Gabriel's unexpected return reawakens Ilona's desire for affection and independence. She must grapple with her emotions and the rigid societal norms binding her in a loveless marriage even while contending with another woman setting her lusty sights on Gabriel.

The discovery of her self-righteous husband's dark secrets forces Ilona to confront the reality of her life. With her world on the brink of implosion, she must find the courage to reclaim her voice, embrace true love, and fully embrace her artistry.

Set in 1949 against the rich backdrop of a small southern town, *Watercolor Whispers* is a poignant exploration of a young woman's struggle to find her voice in a silencing world and her transformative journey of empowerment and self-discovery.

Other Books by This Author

Generation Series

Wandering Beauty – Book 2

Lawrence Family Series

Forever Yours

Fixer Upper Love

Finally Yours

Night Series

Caliente Nights

Sultry Nights

Seductive Nights

Two Hearts as One Series

Baby Love

Trembling Hearts

Mended Hearts

Love at Last Series

It's My Turn

Baby, I'm For Real

Love Conquers All Series

A Special Summer

When Love Comes Around

Key To My Heart

Second Chance At Love

The Sweetest Love

Anthologies

Losing The Bid

Chasing After Love

Wonderful Readers

Thank you for reading Graceful Watercolors. I pray Ella's story of tragedy to triumph resonated with you, as it did with me. If Ella's journey intrigued you, I'm certain you'll enjoy getting to know Ella's great-grandmother, Ilona Robinson-Thurman, in *Watercolor Whispers*, written by Suzette D. Harrison.

Remember, the past intertwines with the present.

Until next time,

Suzette

Let's Connect

Website: Suzette Riddick

Facebook: Author Suzette Riddick

Instagram: Suzette Riddick

Pinterest: Suzette Riddick Books

Acknowledgments

Thank you, God, for your unmerited grace. Your unfailing love is beyond comprehension.

Suzette D. Harrison aka Twin, I'm loving this journey we're on together. Truly, I'm in awe of how Colemanville is materializing into a vibrant southern town. I wouldn't want to be on this journey with anyone else.

Autumn Dorsey, your auntie appreciates you so much. Thank you for being a resource and answering all my questions about the life of an NBA photographer.

Nicole Falls...girl! Having you as an editor these last few years has been AMAZING! Your integrity and work ethic are stellar. I can't express how much I value and appreciate you.

About the Author

Suzette Riddick is a wife, mother, and nurse practitioner who enjoys writing stories about imperfect people finding perfect love. Black love, sisterhood, and strong family bonds are the heart of her stories. She is an Amazon Best-Selling Author and featured in USA Today ~ Happy Ever After. Suzette, a native of Philadelphia, PA, loves traveling, reading, decorating her planner, and has an addiction to Chanel parfum.

Made in the USA
Monee, IL
12 November 2024